MARSHAL HORNE of Talon's Crossing

AIRSHIP 27 PRODUCTIONS

TM

Marshal Horne of Talon's Crossing
All stories © 2021 Tyler Auffhammer

Published by Airship 27 Productions
www.airship27.com
www.airship27hangar.com

Interior illustrations © 2021 Jeff Cram
Cover illustration © 2021 Adam Shaw

Editor: Ron Fortier
Associate Editor: Kimberly Hanson
Marketing and Promotions Manager: Michael Vance
Production Designer: Rob Davis

ISBN: 978-1-953589-15-6

Printed in the United States of America

10 9 8 7 6 5 4 3 2 1

MARSHAL HORNE of Talon's Crossing

TABLE OF CONTENTS

GUN SHOW SCALPERS

With his left hand holding his pistol and his right trying to rip the arrow from his thigh, Cavalryman Tom Stratford reined his pony using his knees as best he could. He followed the empty-saddled pony ahead of him around the back of the barn and saw two Indians drawing back their bows twenty yards ahead. He aimed his pistol and fired once at each, hitting both men in the thick of their bodies. They fell from their ponies.

Stratford reined his mare around and saw two men run from the front porch of the ranch house. One had a rifle and the other had two pistols. They fired at the mass of Indians that rode around their front yard, sent arrows at the house and screamed out curses that followed their flighted arrows. The man with the rifle fell with an arrow to his chest, and the other man, older and heavier, dragged him back under the porch.

Stratford fired his remaining two shots at the brave who'd killed the man, and grazed him enough to send him falling from his pony. Two braves overtook Stratford from behind and he was clubbed in the head. He fell from his horse and onto the ground. His chest ached and he gasped for breath. Slowly the air returned to his lungs. He crawled forward toward the porch. Ponies flew by him and arrows riddled the ground on either side of him. A brave, shirtless and covered in blood, jumped on top of him.

Stratford rolled the Indian over and managed to gain top mount on him. He pulled his belt knife, a stag-handled Bowie, and tried to stab him in the chest. The brave dodged it and kicked Stratford away. The brave was on him again in a flash, and this time wrestled his own bone-handled knife toward Stratford's neck. Stratford craned his neck away and the knife plunged into the soft soil beside it. He plunged a knee into the brave's groin and the Indian fell to the side, but only momentarily.

Stratford punched the Indian hard in the face, then the brave scratched his jaw with his fingernails. Stratford reached for a pistol lying in the dirt, but was kicked in the nose as he did. He fell backward, and grabbed his bleeding nose. The Indian was on him again, never letting up. He clawed and punched at the soldier's head. Stratford felt his vision blurring from

5

the blows. Through the flurry of hand strikes he saw the brave's red face, full of fury and focus. The brave's teeth were clenched and barred like a rabid animal. Suddenly, a shot rang out. The brave fell back dead. The older man from the porch ran to Stratford and pulled him under it to safety.

Stratford watched the remaining braves set fire to the well and surround the barn but the fire would not catch on the wet wood. The ranchers had heard them coming long before they arrived. They could save their barn, but not their lives. The elder cradled the younger man in his lap, and brushed his thick hair away from his cold, dead eyes. Stratford pulled himself up and sat back against the wall of the ranch house. He watched the Indians recede into the distant rolling hills almost as quickly as they had arrived thirty minutes prior, like ethereal ghosts in a sunrise.

✪✪✪

Marshal Gideon Horne and his deputy, Seth Barr, watched the team of covered wagons, mounted riders, and pack mules slowly make their way down Main Street toward the west end of town, where the open field beyond the last building had slowly been filled with tents. It was the slow but altogether rambunctious arrival of Grigson's Gun Show to Talon's Crossing. A time of booming business, technological innovation, and young people aiming to prove they were as good a shot as Wild Bill Hickok or Annie Oakley.

Deputy Barr, wearing just a white shirt and gray waistcoat, caught sight of a wood-covered wagon and spoke up, "You think this is the last of 'em?"

Horne spat into the dust below the Marshal's Office steps. He wore a black vest over a gray shirt. He was fanning his black hat in front of his face. "Yeah, I think so. When they came last time, I remember seeing that wood-covered wagon. I think that's Grigson's wagon."

Horne's assumption proved correct, and the wood-covered wagon stopped in front of the Nest as the rest of the entourage passed by. The wagon resembled a Wells Fargo wagon, possibly a retired service model, because of the wooden covered rear portion, where canvas was usually found. A group of men out front of the Nest slowly walked up beside it. Suddenly, the wooden sides of the wagon burst open and were held up by shims and latches. On the side of the wagon it read: "Grigson's Gun Show: Est. 1870. Silas Grigson, Proprietor." The other sides included advertisements for different weapons, ammunition, and engraving services.

A skinny, well-dressed man with a salt and pepper handlebar mustache jumped out of the wagon. He smiled, looking around for his first financial victim. He quickly realized the volume of townsfolk that had assembled around his wagon and the preceding line that had slowly trickled in over the past ten minutes. His smile broadened from ear to ear.

He hollered out, "Welcome, one and all! I am Silas Grigson, owner/proprietor of Grigson's Gun Show, established 1870 in the Black Hills. I hope all of you have lined your wallets and opened your pockets because Grigson's has all that you've been missing!"

Suddenly, a flock of men folk gathered around Grigson, shaking his hand and asking him questions. Horne recognized a few of them, including Jarron Hyde and Pete Townsend, two young laborers that were always fighting with each other. He wondered when their next skirmish would begin.

"That Grigson sure knows how to get attention," said Barr, spitting his tobacco juice over the railing. He rubbed the raw skin of his freshly shaved face with his palm.

"Yeah, last time he caught the ire of every housewife in the Emerald Valley. Every one of their husbands came home with a new rifle, box of rounds, and no explanation for how they paid for it."

Two riders approached them to the right. Horne looked up and saw Darryl Selby sitting slouched over in his saddle. Beside him, a man dressed in the remains of the US Cavalry uniform sat tall and straight in his saddle. Shelby was owner of the Hooked S Ranch. Horne noticed splotches of dried blood on the front of his shirt. Selby threw something down in front of Horne, who quickly assessed it: three arrows, brightly colored feathers, blood on the heads.

"I pulled those out of my boys," Selby was a hard man, and his voice was deep and guttural like he'd smoked every day of his life.

Horne stepped forward. "I see the bloodshed finally spilled into the Emerald Valley." Recent raids by the Southern Band of the Utes had brought in a strong US Cavalry presence to the area. Back and forth battles between the two forces had spilled over onto citizen's property more than once already. Selby, it seemed, was the first member of Talon's Crossing to feel the sharp sting of war. And his family had paid the price.

"Cavalry led em right onto our property about eleven this morning. We heard the battle about thirty minutes before it arrived. Gave us enough time to load up and douse the barn and ranch house in case of fire."

"My God," Barr gasped. He pulled the tobacco out of his mouth and let it drop over the railing.

The Cavalryman spoke up. "We lost our position pretty quick and the Utes were all over the place, throwing spears and slinging arrows like we'd killed Muatagoci."

Chief Muatagoci was the war chief of the Southern Ute tribe. He'd been the unquestioned leader of their war party for some time and a lot of folks claimed to see him from South Dakota to New Mexico, like he was a specter capable of appearing and re-appearing in any place he liked.

Selby continued. "Tad and Randall got hit first, just outside the barn. They tried to burn the barn, but it wouldn't take because of what we done prior. Then, my boy... Sam... he..."

Selby's voice trailed off amid a stream of fresh tears. Horne assumed what had happened, and didn't prod any further. Suddenly, shooting commenced in the center of town, down to the left from the Marshal's Office. Horne and Barr jumped up and ran down the steps toward the commotion. Selby and the Cavalryman followed on their horses.

When Horne arrived at the circle of people gathered around Grigson's wagon, he placed his hand on the pistol sitting ready in its holster. He pushed by familiar bodies until he reached the gunfire. Barr was close behind him.

"That's mighty fine shootin', sonny, but I think the older gentleman takes the cake on this one," judged Silas Grigson. He wore a fine suit of starched gray cloth, with white pinstripes down each side. Grigson placed a few tokens in the hands of an older man, who Horne recognized as Barry Friedman, the baker. "And, don't forget sir, that those tokens are redeemable at any Grigson's authorized dealer in town."

Horne walked up and stared at Grigson. He was a sight shorter than Horne, and much skinnier. He'd obviously not worked horses or land in his time.

"Hold on, sir," Grigson told Horne. "You'll have to wait your turn." Grigson motioned to a series of targets placed on the side of the wagon. They were nailed to the wooden boards and above them, written in bright red lettering, read: "Bull's Eye Shootin'."

"I've waited long enough," Horne said, grabbing the small pinwheel from Grigson's left hand. "We've got noise ordinances in town for this type of event. We won't have shooting within the limits."

"Marshal Horne," Jarron Hyde, a local boy, spoke up. "We need something to do around here."

"Then find a broom and start pushin' it," Horne suggested.

"Marshal, we ain't got nothing against the town law, but you coming to put a stop to all this seems a bit fishy," accused Pete Townsend.

"What's your game, Pete?"

"I think ole' Jarron Hyde over there put you up to this. To keep me from out-shootin' his yellow belly."

"How dare you..." began Hyde, storming toward Townsend. Barr jumped between them to keep them from fighting.

"Nobody put me up to anything, Pete," Horne stated, half-feeling like the comment didn't even deserve a response.

Grigson, who had remained unexpectedly quiet during the ordeal, walked up to Horne and whispered to his shoulder, "I think there's some way we can work this out, Marshal."

Something touched Horne's belly. He looked down and saw a stack of bills in Grigson's hands. Before Horne could respond, Darryl Selby rode up next to Grigson.

"You men are fools," Selby held the reins tightly on his mare. "Worried about shooting and frolicking when Utes are raiding every farm West of Salt Lake City."

"Utes?" Grigson looked worried for the first time. "Are they armed?"

"With their own brand of weaponry, yes," Selby replied.

"No rifles?" The salesman queried.

"Not yet."

"Then I'll have to make them an offer."

Instantly, Selby reared his pony and she stamped and kicked in place, almost as if meant for Grigson. Horne stepped in front of Grigson to keep him from being knocked cold. When he saw Marshal Horne, Selby calmed the horse.

"What's got you in a fire, Selby?" Pete Townsend asked.

"My goddamn ranch was attacked and my boys murdered!" Selby roared. He fought tears welling in the corners of his eyes.

The mention of death sent a murmur through the crowd of townsfolk gathered around them. Selby hung his body low in the saddle for the first time, the rush of memories too much for him to bear. Horne watched him with precision, trying to calculate his next move. Ahead of him was Silas Grigson, who had rushed to his wagon and returned now with a long, leather gun case.

"Folks of Talon's Crossing," he called out. "Here I've got the solution to all of your problems." Instantly, the townsfolk turned their ears to him, forgetting Selby's plight. Horne noticed Deputy Barr had left and saw him speaking with a man outside the Marshal's Office.

As Grigson slowly opened the case, it revealed a Winchester Model 1886 rifle, with gold-plating on the receiver and trigger guard, along with a carved ivory stock featuring images of buffalo. It was one of the most beautiful guns Horne had ever seen, probably the most expensive gun west of the Mississippi. Grigson picked it up out of the gun case and held it up for all to see. Again, a fire spread through the crowd, this time tinged with greed.

"This here is the limited edition, one-of-a-kind, Winchester Model 1886, with lever action motion and a caliber large enough to take down a buffalo, like the ones carved into that beautiful ivory stock. You'll also notice the gold located throughout the rifle."

"I want that sucker!" Yelled Jarron Hyde.

Pete Townsend shoved past him. "No, it's mine! What do I gotta do?"

"Hold on, gentlemen," Grigson counseled. "'To each his own, in his own time', my mother used to say. This here rifle is an exclusive that has to be won."

"Won?" Townsend scratched his ear.

"How so?" Hyde added.

"In a shooting competition, of course," Grigson grinned. A hum flooded the crowd again. "This shooting competition will play host the finest shooting men and women of the Emerald Valley. Over the next couple of days, I will take entrants into the competition. Then we'll shoot, one target per person, the most shots placed to the bulls-eyes will be declared the winner. And owner of this fine piece of shooting ephemera."

"Sign me up," Hyde stepped forward.

"Hold on, now, partner. There's more to it than that. To make things fair, and to make sure Mr. Winchester gets his due, they'll be an entrant fee of twenty dollars."

"Twenty dollars?" Pete Townsend shook his head. "That's more than most of us make in a few months.

"Which is why I'm giving you a few days to come up with the cash," Grigson clarified. "Or to find a sponsor."

"A sponsor?" Asked Jarron Hyde. "Who would pay for someone else to win a gun?"

"Mr...?"

"Hyde, Jarron Hyde."

"Mr. Hyde, well, you see, this rifle will earn the winner instant celebrity. People will hear about your victory from miles around and you'll be asked to perform at banquets, gallerias, and perhaps even the Governor's Ball."

Horne began to question Grigson's motivation, but silently applauded his efforts. The folks of Talon's Crossing were a good bunch, but a bit out of touch. He watched Townsend and Hyde quarrel now over who they'd ask to sponsor them. Grigson was trying to get the attention of the crowd again, but the thought of fame and fortune was too much for the townsfolk to bear. People began arguing, yelling, some questioned their friendships and matrimonial ties. Everyone wanted that gun, no matter what it took to get it. *Greed*, thought Horne, *was a powerful and fast-acting poison.*

Horne looked back toward the Marshal's Office. The rider had dismounted and stood with Deputy Barr, who motioned for Horne to join them. *Anywhere but here*, Horne thought to himself. These folks would be fame-crazy until this show left town and there was nothing a marshal could change about that. He walked through the crowd and up to his office, where the man beside Barr came into focus.

He was long and lean and looked dusty and dirty— all from long hours in the saddle. His face had a thick, black mustache and his greasy black hair had tendrils that seemed to squirm beneath his gray slouch hat. His eyes, too, were grey, and stared at Horne through the sunlight that permeated the street from its five o'clock position. Horne noticed his silver star pinned to his left lapel and the words "Deputy U.S. Marshal" emblazoned onto the metal. He wore two pistols, both cross draw, on his hips, too.

"Marshal Gideon Horne," Barr did the introductions. "Please meet Cliven Daniels, Deputy U.S. Marshal." Both men shook hands.

"Your name precedes you," said Horne. "Your heroics at the attack on Fort Ruby was in the papers from here to Abilene."

"It was a bloodbath and I was lucky to make it out alive," Daniels had a deep, silky voice.

"Spoken like a true peace officer," Horne nodded. "Please, come in."

The three lawmen stepped across the threshold of Horne's office and took seats around his desk. Daniels started a cigarette using a match he lit with the seam of his pants.

"I take it you're aware of the recent increase in raiding activity by the Southern Paiute Indians, led by Chief Muatagoci." He drew long on his smoke.

"Yes," said Horne. "In fact, one of those men out there just rode in from his ranch. His sons are dead, and he's lucky to have a house still standing."

"Yeah," added Barr. "And his barn..."

Daniels cut off the deputy. "The Federal Judge down in Reno sent me up to the Emerald Valley to help quell the increasing aggression of these Utes. He's got an eye on Muatagoci and wants the War Chief taken down. So does the Governor. They suspect Muatagoci is trying to start a rebellion."

"Really?" Horne sat up straight. "They think we should be seeing more of this? Are the troops not making headway?"

Daniels was staring out the front window now, smoking on his cigarette. He blew a puff of smoke onto the glass. "From the look of that young soldier out on your porch, I think not."

"He was fending off the Indians with the rancher," Barr explained.

Daniels looked at him, then puffed a nonchalant ball of smoke. He looked toward Horne. "We need to start fortifying the town in case Muatagoci comes this way."

"You think that's a possibility?"

Barr butted in. "Marshal, there's no way the Ute raiding parties would dare attack a fully supplied town. Let alone one with a gun competition going on."

Just then, a few shots went off down the street. All three men disregarded the noise. It was illegal to fire shots within town limits, but Marshal Horne suspected every city councilman was at the gun show and it would be difficult to explain the arrest of the proprietor, or the marksmen, to anyone. Horne rubbed his jaw. The Utes were powerful, but, like Barr suggested, he doubted they'd come after Talon's Crossing. Before the Indian Wars broke out, Talon and his family had good relations with the Natives in the Emerald Valley. For the most part, they stayed out of each other's way. Now, though, with the Cavalry running them down, the Utes might just seek a bigger prize.

Just then, Darryl Selby walked in through the front door. The soldier was with him. Selby took his hat off and held it between his fingers.

"I'll be headin' back now to see about my property. And my sons' graves. Marshal," he sidled up to Horne in a way to keep the next words between just the two of them, "Those Utes wanted blood, plain and simple. I think it'd be best you start alerting folks around here to fortify and stay inside, until the Cavalry can run 'em out."

The soldier stepped forward, having heard the comment. "I will be returning to Fort Carlin tomorrow and telling my superiors about your problem up here. We were chasing Northern Utes to this southern region and not expecting they'd receive reinforcements from their Southern brothers, let alone Muatagoci himself. Believe me, sir, we'll be back to avenge our fallen. Hopefully before any more white blood is spilt."

Horne nodded and shook each man's hand. Selby and the soldier, whose name Horne couldn't recall, left without another word. Daniels, who'd finished his smoke and stuffed it out on the window sill, turned to look at Horne.

"I think it's best you and I sit down and talk fortifications for Talon's Crossing. I don't know the terrain as well as I used to, and a lot of new ranches and farms have cropped up, but you can help with that."

"I agree, Daniels."

Barr jumped in again. "Marshal, we need to start alerting people, like Selby said."

"No," Daniels protested. "We've got to protect this town first. The majority of residents of this valley live in town, especially the resourceful ones."

"What's that mean?"A bemused look crossed Deputy Barr's face.

"The bankers and land agents and councilman live here, son," Daniels continued. "And the papers don't take kindly to good citizens bein' scalped. A rancher or two, maybe, but not a banker."

"You and your federal status, Daniels, can go straight to hell," cursed Barr. "And don't you dare talk down about those ranchers. They're just as good men as any, an' better than some!"

Daniels stepped forward, but Horne stepped between them. Horne was taller than Daniels and stockier. Daniels backed down. He pulled cigarette fixings out of his vest and began again. Horne slowly turned to his deputy.

"Look, Seth, if you think we should start alerting folks, I understand. You're your own man now more than ever. I'll give you leave to follow your nose. With Marshal Daniels here, I think we're set."

Barr was surprised by Horne's parting words. Barr resented Daniels' arrival. It angered him to see the sway that the US Marshal had already taken over Horne. Barr shoved his hat on his head and left, content to ride the fringes of the Emerald Valley until Daniels found the trail again.

Once Barr left, Daniels commented, "Quite a spitfire you got there."

"He's a damn good deputy."

"No doubt," Daniels watched the deputy ride away from town through the window. "Now, let's get to work."

"Marshal! Marshal! Open up, Marshal!"

The voice outside Horne's Marshal Office window was loud and uninviting. It leaned on the side of plain obtrusive. But Marshal Horne, who'd been up until the wee hours of the palely lit prairie dawn, managed to lift himself from the jail cot and get to the door.

"Horne! Marshal Horne!" The voice yelled again.

Horne sidestepped the pile of ammo boxes he'd pushed to the center of the office and opened the door. Autumn was already setting in, he could tell from the rush of ghostly cold wind that slipped through the doorway. Standing outside was Silas Grigson, proprietor. Horne and Daniels had worked all night on their plans for fortifying Talon's Crossing, and Horne caught a few glimpses of Grigson and his wagon party across the street. Grigson was still buttering up pliable townsfolk for his turkey shoot in the coming days.

"Marshal, thank God you're up," Grigson said in a rush. Behind Grigson stood a large, dark-skinned man who at least half-Indian but wore a suit of fine wool better than Horne's. He suspected he was an associate, or worse, an employee, of Grigson.

"What's to do?" Horne covered his bare chest with the blanket still draped around his shoulders.

"My rifle's been stolen," Grigson pushed his way into the office and then he plopped down in Deputy Barr's chair.

"What rifle?"

"The prized rifle for my shooting competition, Marshal," said Grigson, who quickly suspected that Horne had forgotten about it, but also never missed a chance to brag on his accoutrements, "Ivory stocked Model 1886, straight from Winchester factory in New Haven, complete with gold fittings and buffalo…"

"Yes, yes," said Horne, "I know now, thanks."

"Well, I woke this morning and it's gone."

"Have you checked around? Maybe you left it somewhere?"

"No, sir, I don't hardly handle that gun," Grigson looked back at his compadre. "It stays locked in a secure gun box in the back of my main wagon. I have the key right here." Grigson displayed a small brass key, complete with the Winchester logo engraved in the top portion.

"Was the box broken into?"

"That's what's odd about it, Marshal— no. No tampering, no breaking of the lock. It's like I opened it in my sleep, hid it away, and then locked everything back up."

"No other keys?"

"None."

"My rifle's been stolen!"

"No one else had access to this key?"

"Nope, I keep it attached to my watch fob," Grigson reminded himself. He pulled a large, gold watch from his vest pocket. It was an open-faced model with large, black hands that slowly ticked around thanks to the ephemeral power of yesterday's wind up. He clipped the key back onto a ring that was suspended to the watch's bow and then placed it back into his vet pocket. Horne noted its position.

"So what am I to do, Marshal? That's a prized gun."

"Well," Horne poured himself a cup of cold coffee and stoked the embers of the wood-burning stove next to the jail cells. "You made sure everyone in town knew about it and saw it yesterday, so the suspect list is kind of long at this point. Anyone take a keen eye to it more than the rest?"

The big man standing behind Grigson spoke up for the first time. "Those two men sure were eyeing it up, Mr. Grigson." He had a deep voice that Horne could tell was still unsure of the noises it made, like a puppy who just found his bark.

"Who, Anson?"

"The young men, who wanted to fight each other," Anson elaborated.

"Townsend and Hyde, I believe," Horne confirmed. He set his cup on top of the now hot wood stove to warm. "They're rowdy, but thieves? I don't know."

"Well, would you look into it?" Grigson all but begged.

"I will. But I've got a band of Ute Indians roaming around that may prove to be a bigger problem than your missing gun, no offense. I will do my best."

"Thank you."

Grigson and Anson both moved to leave through the front door. As Anson left, Horne stopped Grigson with his words.

"I wouldn't let anyone know about this Grigson. I don't mean to involve myself, but if you let them know that gun is gone, you may lose your crowd."

"Thank you. And if that crowd has nothing on which to spend their time, you may lose your town, Marshal."

With that, Grigson left. A few moments passed and Horne picked up his now bubbling cup of coffee. He blew on it and let the steam roll from the edges of the tin cup.

✪✪✪

The next few days brought considerable improvements to the town's fortifications. Horne worked spreading ammunition among the town's businessmen. Many of them protested the actual threat level of the Utes, as their attacks seem to occur only on outlying ranches and settlements, but at Horne's behest they abided by his decision. Daniels, meanwhile, began stocking the front and back doors of the buildings with buckets of water, in case of an attack with fire. Deputy Barr remained gone for the entire day, while Horne and Daniels worked tirelessly themselves, making changes to their plans as they saw fit but overall feeling a sense of accomplishment at the protections so far.

On the second day, Deputy Seth Barr arrived mid-morning on horseback, with a rider accompanying him. Horne and Daniels stood on the front porch of the Marshal's Office, drinking coffee and preparing for their day of work. Grigson, meanwhile, was down the street, preparing for his shooting competition. He'd not approached Horne about his missing rifle all the day prior, and for that Horne was appreciative. He made a mental note to ask around about it, if he found the time.

As Barr approached the front of the office, Horne noticed the other man was Frankie Lange, a lean and long man from the Crooked Coyote Ranch on the southern pasture. Lange was bloody on his right arm, his shirt half-torn from his body, and wore no boots. He held a long Winchester rifle in his left hand. Horne stepped down from his perch on the office porch.

"What happened, Frankie?"

"Marshal, those god-damned Indians killed my Pa."

Horne sucked in his breath and held it in his barrel chest. He'd suspected another Ute attack wouldn't be far behind the Selby raid, but to hear that Joe Lange was gone angered him to no avail. Lange and Horne were Emerald Valley natives and tried their hand at a run-down school as boys, also to no avail. Lange was a strong man, but became withered in his old days. To know these young Ute braves preyed on him was a cruel move.

"When?" Asked Daniels, interrupting.

Lange did not respond, but hung his head and sobbed.

Barr spoke up. "An hour ago. The sun came bursting up and so did they. Luckily I was rounding the bend in the trail and saw the attack begin. I managed to match up with Frankie and repel a lot of the brunt force of the raid, but his dad couldn't get to us. His legs... But that's not the worst of it."

"What's worse?" Horne did his best to quell his anger.

"They were headed here when we left, maybe fifteen minutes ago."

The thought of the Utes on their way here sent chills down Horne's spine. An angry war band of young, skilled warriors against a town full of people more focused on some damn shooting competition than their own well-being. *They'd have their shooting, that's for sure*, thought Horne. *It would be a matter of life and death before the end.*

"We need to continue the fortifications and expedite the plan, Marshal," Daniels stated the obvious as he lit a cigarette.

"No," Barr disagreed. "We need to convince the rest of the outlying ranches and farms to come into Talon's Crossing for backup."

"You think they'll leave?" Daniels retorted. "Did that old cripple leave?"

"You shut your damned mouth!" Frankie Lange said, lifting a finger.

"Daniels is right," Horne nodded. "Those ranchers won't leave their herds to come protect a few buildings and townsfolk."

"If we ride out together they might," Barr argued. "It's our only hope. You know we can't protect this town from a band of raiding Indians. They're too many."

"Hence the fortifications," added Daniels.

Barr got down from his horse and walked up to Daniels. Daniels, who was now puffing on his cigarette, straightened up and stared at Barr, who was shorter and scrawny compared to his own physique. Barr glared at him, but then removed his face from Daniels' and turned to Marshal Horne.

Barr leaned close and whispered. "Marshal, you can't take this man's advice. He's not from here, he doesn't know who these people are or what they'll do."

"I understand that, but I think you're letting jealousy cloud your vision here, Deputy." The inclusion of Barr's official title gave Horne's words a didactic tone. Barr was taken aback and shook his head, disapprovingly. Horne's next words were loud enough for all to hear, "But I do like Barr's idea about reinforcements. If we can get some help from the U.S. Cavalry on this, maybe from Fort McDermott?" Horne looked at Daniels.

"You want me to send a telegram?"

"That'd be a start," Deputy Barr snapped.

Daniels took affront with Barr's tone, throwing his cigarette down and marching up to the deputy. He added, "You better watch that tone with me, Deputy, or I'll arrest you."

"You gonna put me in my own jail?"

"I'll put you in your place."

"Alright, gentlemen," Horne forcefully pushed himself between the two. "We need some time apart. Daniels, send that telegram to Fort McDermott, being very detailed on the situation we're in. Barr, I think you and Frankie should try to round up Selby and his crew to convince the ranchers to come back to town and give help where it's needed. Hell, even ten to fifteen men would be a big help."

Horne turned and ascended the steps, disappearing into his office. After stomping out his lit cigarette, Daniels followed Horne into the building, glancing back at Barr as he did. Frankie Lange and Seth Barr turned their mounts around and headed toward the end of town. At the end, however, Barr turned back and caught a glimpse of Daniels leaving the office with a square of telegram paper in his hand. Barr's eyes followed Daniels' route to the telegraph office past the Nest. Barr knew the telegraph operator, Sonny, was not in the office on Mondays. It was his fishing day. Yet, Daniels disappeared into the small building, and returned without the telegram. Something inside Barr turned sour. It was the same inclination that had prompted Marshal Horne to hire such a young and inexperienced deputy.

As Daniels disappeared back into the Marshal's Office, Barr turned to Frankie Lange, who was waiting to head out. "Wait here, I gotta run back to the telegraph office. I forgot something."

Barr raced his pony past the Marshal's Office, looking in the window as he did, in case someone was watching him. There was no face in the square glass. He continued on past the Nest, where he saw a flock of men inside talking and eating, until his horse came to a stop outside the telegraph office. Barr dismounted and entered the building.

Inside was a stockpile of tree corpses. Papers were stacked on every surface, ranging from old newspapers to new, blank telegram stock. While it was cluttered, everything looked to be organized into square stacks, each in its own place. How everything should be, Barr thought. He searched the main desk, where he figured Daniels' would have dropped the new telegram. Nothing. He searched a few adjacent stacks and open trays, but did not see anything addressed to Fort McDermott. Just as he turned to leave, he focused on the trash can that sat beside the desk next to the front door.

The can was half full of old food and crinkled papers. As Barr approached, however, he saw a freshly folded piece of white, square telegram stock paper. He reached down and picked it up. In pencil scratchings, it read: "To: Fort McDermott, East Fork, Quinn River, Nevada Territory. From: U.S. Deputy Marshal Cliven Daniels. Subject: Indian Raids." The main body of the telegraph did not say anything. In fact, there were two lines of scribbling that looked as if a schoolboy had done them. Nothing legible. Definitely not a plea for help. In that moment, Barr realized Daniels' treachery ran deep. He'd suspect the man wasn't on the on the level, but now it was true. He had no intentions of seeing Talon's Crossing survive these raids. For what reason, though, Barr couldn't figure.

As Barr left the office and mounted his pony, he contemplated telling Horne. Showing him the blank telegram, but thought better. Daniels was a sly talker and would have a handy excuse. Horne, for some reason, looked past the obvious sometimes, when he was busy in thought with protecting the people of Emerald Valley. Barr admired that in his boss, but also saw its flaws. As Barr passed the Marshal's Office, he realized the only thing he could do was round up as much support he could and hope he made it back in time to help his friends. As he met Frankie Lange at the edge of town, they picked up their pace and headed Easterly toward the Selby ranch.

✪✪✪

"Step right up, gentlemen and lady, and put your money where your mouth is," proclaimed Grigson, standing behind a table covered in a bright blue tablecloth. On the front of the fabric, it read, in gilded letters: "Grigson's Emerald Valley Shootout."

A long line had begun to form around Grigson's wagon train starting at eight o'clock in the morning. Among them, Jarron Hyde and Pete Townsend, who incurred the headlong stare of Anson, Grigson's right-hand-man. Pete and Jarron had each managed to scrounge their twenty dollar entrance fee and placed it on the table. A young dove, recruited from her perch in the Nest, took their money and began writing down their information.

"Townsend," Hyde chided. "You'll be lucky to hit the broadside of the damn barn today. I see you shaking from all that coffee."

"And you'll be lucky if I don't use you for target practice," Townsend snickered back.

"Gentlemen, gentlemen," Grigson raised his arms. "Take it easy. You've paid your fee, and you'll get your chance to shoot, just like everyone else. Remember, that gilded rifle is up for grabs."

Pete and Jarron exited the line and took their place against the side wall of the abandoned Methodist church, which had become vacant only in the last few months after the pastor, Chester Kolb, had passed in his sleep. Grigson was using the church as the backdrop for the shooting competition, so that bullets wouldn't tear through occupied buildings. Grigson's crew of four to five men had worked diligently all morning setting up the banners, flags, and targets on the wooden building. There were eight targets set up for the eight entrants to the competition.

Along with Hyde and Townsend, six other people had managed to pay the entrance fee: Dan Speedman, the local barber and one of the crack shots of the Emerald Valley. Most of the businessmen in town had helped pay his entrance fee, with the understanding that, when he won, he'd place the rifle up above the bar at the Nest. Eden Williams, an out-of-towner who'd brought with him the remnants of a gold claim in the Black Hills. He was banking on selling the rifle when he won. Lorin Stewart, a local rancher's son who had more money than ability, but his father was proud to pay his fee, despite this shortcoming. Jessie and Jordan Peterson, two former War veterans who ran a small dairy farm just north of town and were known far-and-wide for their familial rivalries. This seemed to be another step in their way toward a blood feud. Finally, Lady Alice Nordish. A transplant from the frigid tundra of Norway some years ago, Lady Nordish was the heiress of a great fortune, thanks to her father, but was drawn to the Emerald Valley's beauty. No one knew of Nordish's abilities with a gun. In the wake of his wife's death some years ago, the townsfolk attempted matrimonial subterfuge between Horne and Nordish to no avail.

After the group finished paying their entrance fees, Grigson took center stage near the abandoned church porch. A crowd of at least fifty people had gathered around the wagons and were now quickly flooding the front stoop around Grigson. The eight competitors stood front and center, each with their hands on their hips, ready for battle. Grigson was handed a crude megaphone by Anson, who swiftly stepped out of the spotlight.

"Ladies and gentlemen of the Emerald Valley, residents of Talon's Crossing, are you ready for the greatest feats of cartridge shooting of your lifetime?"

The crowd responded to Grigson's words with a general applause that steadily increased to a crescendo and then plummeted when he began again.

"Today, we have brought you eight of the finest shooters in the Emerald Valley and beyond. Among them, Pete Townsend, Jarron Hyde, two young up-and-comers ready to make their proverbial mark on the world. Dan Speedman, who's better with a gun than he is with shears. Eden Williams, of Black Hills with a claim to fame and who is eager to add the prize rifle to his stock of gold. Lorin Stewart, who is hoping to step from his father's shadow and prove his own mettle in this competition. Brothers Peterson, who seek to break apart the family ties that bind them and see who, finally, is the better of the two. And, finally, from the far and away fields of Norway, Lady Alice Nordish, who, whether she wins or loses, has pledged to buy a round for all onlookers at the bar afterward!"

The final statement received quite a stir from the crowd. As the pitch of the group finally subsided, Marshal Horne managed to find a moment to arrive on the scene, as well. Daniels was busy prepping the livery stable with a wagon, just in case the town fell and they needed to make a run for it. He'd been loading it down with supply barrels as a defense against arrows. Horne had told him he'd be back after watching the competition for a bit.

"And now, let's get to shooting!" Directed Grigson, waving his arm as he jumped down from the porch and walked to the side of the building. He motioned for the eight competitors to take their places against the far wall of Ms. Fink's Restaurant, opposite the empty church, where the eight targets, in this case eight Indian portraits, were nailed up. Grigson's crew brought out eight brand new Winchester repeating rifles. The extra-long sharpshooting barrels were shiny from polish and the wood stocks were checkered for grip in the shoulder.

"These Winchester arms came directly from New Haven this past month and will provide an equal playing field for our eight competitors," Grigson continued as the townsfolk boxed in the shooters on either side of the buildings. "If anything goes wrong with your weapons or your ammunition, which we'll hand out now, please do not hesitate to tell us."

Horne positioned himself against the wall of Ms. Fink's and crossed his arms. He couldn't help but be entranced by the spectacle of it all. He was a townsman at the core of it, and something like this didn't happen often in Talon's Crossing. He watched the competitors load up a single cartridge into the rifles and then place them beside their leg.

"So, the way this will work is each competitor will get one shot. Closest to the bulls-eye on the chest wins round one. That person will be entitled to a free steak dinner at Ms. Fink's, courtesy of Ms. Fink herself," Grigson pointed to a heavy set woman with dark blonde curls. She smiled and waved to the crowd, who slowly clapped for her.

"At the end of the round, we'll take the top four shooters to round two. After that, the top two shooters advance to the final round. Then, we'll crown our winner. So, at the behest of our better manners, Lady Nordish, you'll go first."

Lady Nordish was an older woman, but had retained much of the grace and elegance of her privileged youth. It was obvious she'd been a stunning woman in her youth, and had aged gracefully, like a fine port wine. She wore a white cotton dress that hugged her torso and then ballooned outward toward her legs. Horne thought about their dinner together some years ago and lamented at not pursuing it further. She was a lovely woman, but their lives were very different and they had both realized that in one sitting.

Nordish held up her rifle and pointed it downrange at the Indian who stared back at her with a face full of rage and bared teeth. He carried a tomahawk in one hand and a large Bowie knife in the other. He wasn't wearing anything resembling the local natives, however, but a traditional deerskin loincloth and no shirt. The whites of his eyes had been painted red. As Nordish steadied her gun, the crowd went silent. Everyone watched in eager anticipation. Even Horne found his chest heavy with a saved breath.

Then, she fired. The shot blew a large hole in the Indian's chest, just above the bulls-eye. The sound the gun made ricocheted through the alleyway between the buildings, rattling off everything as it dissipated into the Emerald Valley. A few children covered their ears and somewhere a baby started crying. After walking up and checking her shot, one of Grigson's men held up two fingers to show how far the shot had been from the bulls-eye. Lady Nordish put her rifle back to the ground with a stifled smirk on her face.

Dan Speedman was next, and placed his shot just to the right of the bulls-eye, a hair closer than Nordish's shot. Everyone suspected Speedman would do the best, and he was proving them right. Townsfolk thought him a cocky man, and his large smile and the subtle nodding of his head didn't help to dispel the rumors. Horne recalled seeking a "trim" at his shop, only to receive a bowl cut that made him look like a schoolboy again. Speedman said it "suited" Horne's round physique. Horne hadn't been back yet.

Eden Williams and Lorin Stewart both hit their target, but nowhere near the bulls-eye. Williams' scoured the edge of the target and the wall, while Stewart's nicked the top of the brave's head. Both were visibly disappointed in their performances. The Peterson brothers were next, but argued who should go first. Jessie's plea was that he was younger by three minutes, so his brother should go first. On the other hand, Jordan argued that he was taller, and thus the shorter of two should begin. Grigson settled this debate by forcing them to go at the same time. As many suspected, both brother's shots were damn near equal, but well south of the Indian's chest.

Finally, the heated rivalry took center stage with Pete Townsend and Jarron Hyde, who gave each other headlong glances as they prepared for their shots. Townsends' rivaled Nordish and Speedman's, but was a bit further away from the center. Hyde, meanwhile, was having a time steadying his rifle, and made sure to complain that the barrel seemed "heavier than usual." His shot was awry and nicked the Indian's neck.

At the end round one, Grigson stepped back into the center of the shooting range and spoke. "Well folks, we have a round one winner: Mr. Speedman!"

The crowd clapped for him as he raised his rifle above his head like a victorious warrior.

"Mr. Speedman, congratulations. You may request your free steak dinner at Ms. Fink's within the next calendar year."

"I'd like to offer a seat accompanying me to Ms. Nordish," Speedman bowed gallantly. "At my expense, of course."

Nordish curtsied to him, but did not respond.

"Now, let me announce the four lucky—I mean, deserving— competitors to round two. After much deliberation, my team has concluded that the following list of competitors will get another chance at the prize rifle: Mr. Speedman, of course, Lady Nordish, whose own shot rivaled his, Pete Townsend, and, by a very, very close margin, Jarron Hyde!"

The crowd ravenously clapped for their four winners, especially those that supported one of the four in particular. The four that didn't qualify handed their empty rifles off to Grigson's men and took a spot among the rest of the crowd. Before Grigson began again, the four qualifiers were given another single cartridge. Horne watched them load up their rifles and place them at their feet. Just then, he remembered the missing gun. The event wouldn't take much longer and then a winner would need to receive the rifle. He wondered what Grigson would say about it. Without any leads, Horne would be shooting in the dark. He was content to continue watching. At any rate, things like this had a way of playing themselves out if you held off a little while.

"Alright, folks, let the next round begin!" Shouted Grigson, now using the megaphone again. "We have four skilled competitors who are eager to prove their first round was not a fluke. The top two shots will advance to the final round. The best shot of this round will receive five free boxes of ammunition courtesy of the general store owned by Mr. Jacob Pendergast.

Lady Nordish, since you went first last time, I will give you the option of going last. What do you say?"

"No," she said, in a stern yet elegant voice, "I will prove myself first again and let these boys play from behind."

"You got it," Grigson stepped out of her way.

Nordish lifted her gun and let it steady on her shoulder. Horne could tell she was a practiced sharpshooter. He wondered where she learned the skill and when she honed it. He couldn't remember any conflicts in Norway, nor would he assume to know anything about the place, really. He watched her chest expand and compress slower, slower, until she let out one final breath, squeezed the trigger, and the shot went off.

By now, the town strays had realized more gunshots were to come, so they barked at the latest addition to the cacophony. Lady Nordish's rifle barrel expelled a thick fog of gunpowder smoke as Grigson's man went up to check the shot. When the smoke cleared, the crowd made out a one inch difference between her shot and the bulls-eye. She smiled and placed her rifle next to her leg, as if this were all her normal routine. Grigson commenced clapping, followed by the surrounding townsfolk.

Next up was Speedman, who wasted no time lifting his rifle and pulling off a quick yet accurate shot. It was plain to see he was showing off for Nordish, counteracting her elongated shot process with his short burst of firepower. His shot was similar, but to the left of the bulls-eye, as hers was to the right. He smiled, and the crowd, led specifically by the business owners of town, let out a series of hoops and hollers. It was obvious that Townsend and Hyde would need to be perfect in order to make it to the next round.

Townsend went first to much anticipation, but his shot was a disappointment. It was far and to the left of the brave entirely. Hyde snickered at the shot, and Townsend was visibly disturbed at having committed such a heinous shot. Hyde stepped forward with his loaded rifle, lifted his firearm, and shot. He was confident in his aim, but when Grigson's man returned with a six inch difference in his shot and the bulls-eye, he lowered his head in defeat. Hyde and Townsend shook hands afterward, but were forced to hand over their guns as the eliminated competitors.

"There you have it!" Grigson boomed over the megaphone, "Our two final competitors: Mr. Speedman and Missus, I mean, Lady Nordish. Congratulations to Lady Nordish, as she was the best shot of this round. She'll take home five boxes of cartridges, whether she wins or loses. I'm

Nordish lifted her gun and let it steady on her shoulder.

sure a prize rifle to use those cartridges with would make her happy, though." Lady Nordish smiled.

"Alright," Grigson continued amiably. "Let's move onto our third and final round. Gentlemen, will you please remove the targets." Suddenly, a murmur rose among the crowd about the removal of the targets.

"What will they shoot at?" an old time asked.

"Yeah, I've heard of hitting the broadside of a barn, but not a church," joked another.

Two of Grigson's employees returned with small, square cut sheets of paper. They quickly nailed them to the wall to reveal the tiny face of a Sioux war chief in full eagle feather headdress. He was stoic and emotionless, as most chiefs were assumed to be among church-going folk. Nordish and Speedman were visibly uncomfortable at the new target, but neither let it show to the crowd.

"Now, we have an added challenge for our competitors. An eight by eight sheet of paper, with the bulls-eye now being on the forehead of the chief there. As always, the closest shot will take the victory. As you all know, the prize for winning this round is the eternal gratitude and compliment of Grigson's Gun Show, as well as the men and women of the Emerald Valley." Grigson's voice trailed off.

As expected, another murmur, this time more worried, arose in the group of townsfolk. They were whispering and hushing one another, with a general feeling of angst and anxiety flooding through the crowd.

"And," Grigson continued after a long pause, "the prize rifle, of course!"

Everyone hollered and clapped, relieved to hear the winner would receive the real prize, after all.

Jarron Hyde spoke up, "Where is it?"

Grigson deflected the question and continued his spiel about the competition and the rifle's value and so on.

Pete Townsend joined in. "Yeah, where's the rifle?"

The rest of the crowd echoed their sentiments and Grigson was forced to explain, "The rifle is currently secured in my main wagon, inside the locked box that the Winchester Company shipped it to me in. When we have a winner, they will receive the key and be allowed to retrieve the gun."

Horne wondered how all that would go. He suspected there might be some more than angry people at the sight of the empty Winchester box. Especially the winner. He suspected, if Lady Nordish won, that she would gracefully accept the thought of her prize being stolen, but still expect to be paid the valued price by Grigson. On the other hand, if Speedman won, he might get a full scale riot from the business owners of Talon's Crossing. He secretly rooted for Lady Nordish.

"Alright, seeing as Lady Nordish went first every time, I am going to require that Mr. Speedman begin this time, to make things fair and equal," Grigson said justifying the order in which the finalists would shoot.

With that, Speedman retrieved the cartridge from Grigson's man, loaded it into the rifle, and quickly, without hesitation, lifted the gun and fired. He had confidence, thought Horne, even if his shot didn't find its mark. The smoke cleared and Grigson himself went to check the shot mark. When he turned around, he smiled, and held up two fingers that revealed less than an inch of difference. The entire crowd went into a frenzied state of clapping, cheering, and patting Speedman on the back. He smiled, too, and handed the rifle back to Grigson, as if his work here was done.

Then, the crowd hushed as Lady Nordish stepped forward to receive her cartridge. She'd have to hit the bulls-eye dead on to win this competition and keep the prize rifle out of the hands of Dan Speedman, master marksman and bowl cutter. She slid the brass cartridge into the loading gate with efficiency, cocked the lever, and took a deep breath into her chest. Everyone went silent. Even the stray dogs, who'd begun their howls again when the crowd went wild for Speedman, had found their silence. She lifted the gun, and slowly began her practiced routine of deep breathing.

Just then, Horne caught the sound of a whooping Indian. He scrunched his eyes closer at the target picture of a Sioux war chief, thinking he'd gone mad and started hearing things. The sound grew louder, and Grigson himself began looking around at the faces in the crowd to see who was trying to undermine Lady Nordish's shot. Soon, the war whooping grew to a fever pitch and the sound of horses' thundering hooves joined in the refrain. The crowd of townsfolk looked around, confused and curious. Then, Horne realized their predicament.

The marshal turned, pulled his pistol from his hip holster, and shot a fast-approaching Ute brave who was bearing down on him from the east side of the street. As he did, the townsfolk who did carry weapons, pulled them from their holsters and ran to Horne's aid. A slew of Ute warriors was coming from the east side, but the bark of a dog on the west side alerted them to another attack coming from that direction as well.

All hell broke loose. The braves overtook the townsfolk from all sides. People scattered every which way, seeking shelter where they could: inside buildings, under porches, and behind other people. Dogs ran to and fro, scurrying under legs and barking as they fled. Children were swept into the tense arms of their parents and bystanders to keep from being crushed by the Indians' ponies.

Meanwhile, Horne was picking off as many as he could, joined in doing so by Anson, Mr. Speedman, and Lady Nordish. When Horne's pistol clicked empty, he made a beeline to the other side of the street, hoping to regain some of the lost ground. As he did so, he thought of Deputy Marshal Daniels, alone in the livery. Horne knew he needed more firepower to repel this raid, so he sprinted toward the backdoor of the Marshal's Office and burst inside.

Inside his office, he holstered his pistol and scurried to the gun case, where a Henry rifle was waiting for him. Horne felt a presence behind him, and turned to see a Ute brave gaining ground on him, armed with a tomahawk. Horne lifted the Henry and pulled the trigger, but it was empty. The brave tackled Horne and they fell back over his desk, throwing his office accoutrement across the floor.

Horne got to his feet, but the warrior was on him again, this time trying to hack down on his skull. Horne still had the rifle, so he used it to block the attack and the tomahawk blade lodged itself in the walnut stock of the Henry rifle. Horne threw the gun and blade aside and punched the brave right in the mouth. The brave fell backward, but bounced back at it with precision, taking him down hard on the ground. The brave pulled a sheath knife from his leather belt, raised it, and was shot dead from behind by a pistol. The Indian fell hard beside Horne, who looked up to see Anson holding a smoking gun.

"I saw him follow you," Anson said in his guttural tone. "We need more guns."

Anson and Horne worked quickly to grab the two rifles and shotgun, load them up, and run out the front door. In the street lay a slew of dead white men and women, alongside an equal number of dead Utes. Horne threw a rifle down to Silas Grigson, who turned and began firing off shots in rapid succession, easily proving he had the skills to be running a gun show. Anson took control of the shotgun and let loose double-barrel slugs that blew a Ute brave nearly in half as he ran toward them.

As he fired, Horne realized they'd done an exceptional job at surviving the initial brunt of the attack. Most Indian raids lasted only a few minutes, and were either won or lost in that miniscule amount of time. The raiding party had not accounted for a shooting competition going on when they attacked. The proximity to a stash of rifles and ammunition gave the townsfolk a considerable edge in defending themselves. As two more braves were shot from their ponies, Horne stepped forward into the street.

He hollered out, "Everyone, get inside. Reload your guns and start preparing for another wave of the attack."

Horne, Anson, and Grigson ran inside the Marshal's Office, closed the door behind them, and began covering the windows with anything they could. Grigson started reloading the rifle in his hands and Anson took up defending the back door in case of a sneak attack.

"Marshal," Grigson commented dryly. "Your town sure knows how to welcome an outsider."

"Yeah," Horne replied. "And we sure know how to keep you from coming back."

Grigson laughed. "Say, where's your deputy? And that federal marshal? We could use some more firepower, especially experienced firepower."

Horne wondered the same. He moved the empty ammo box that he'd stuffed into the window and peered down the street toward the livery. He didn't see Daniels. Horne wondered about Barr, too, and whether he would even be on his way back to town or not. It was a long shot, really.

"We sent a telegram to Fort McDermott two days ago, so they may be sending a troop this way, if we're lucky."

"And if we're not lucky?" Asked Anson.

"Then they aren't sending anybody and we have to repel this attack on our own," Horne stated the obvious.

Just then, the next attack began. The repetitive sound of hooves on dirt reached their ears. Still looking through the window, Horne saw a group of at least ten braves coming down the east side of the street, shooting at anything that moved and some that didn't. Among those on horseback, he caught a brightly-dressed old man wearing a pair of dark woven braids, with a large beaded necklace around his chest. He carried a repeating rifle and two pistols on his belt. He suspected this was Chief Muatagoci, from the descriptions of other Ute chieftains he'd heard about.

"We got a problem," Grigson was looking out of the window on the other side of the office. "There's about twenty Indians heading from this side of town."

"Same over here," Horne echoed. "And it looks like Muatagoci is with them."

"Who?"

"Their war chief, Muatagoci. He banded the Southern Utes tribes together against the U.S. Cavalry. He's been raiding settlements in the Emerald Valley for months."

"Why are we just now hearing this?" Grigson was clearly irked.

"We've been fortifying the town for days now, but you've been too busy with the gun show to realize it."

Horne saw a brave holding an arrow lit on the end by a ball of embers. The brave raised his bow and fired the flaming arrow into the hotel across the street. Horne worried it might catch fire.

"Anson, if they try to catch this office on fire, there's a bucket of water near that door. Use it."

Anson nodded.

"I'm leaving," Horne started for the front door.

"What?" Grigson blurted out, surprised. "You can't leave."

"I need to get to the livery. Either Daniels is pinned down or he's injured. Either way, he needs help."

"We all do," countered Grigson.

"Yeah, but he's the best damn gunner we got in this town."

"I beg to differ," Grigson raised his rifle.

"You two hold em off for me. I'm running directly across the street and using the porches to hide all the way to the livery."

Anson and Grigson nodded, reluctantly. Horne recognized the worry in their eyes. He had to go, despite it. He opened the door, waited for two braves to cross by his path, and then ran. He heard gunshots from behind him, thanks to Grigson and Anson. Horne was soon the target of more than one Ute Indian, but he managed to scurry beneath the Nest porch before they got to him. Horne wasted no time crawling beneath the porch in the dirt and cobwebs, and made it to the opening. He waited for his moment, then ran across the divide in the buildings to the hotel.

Horne lifted himself onto the hotel's porch, fetched the barrel of water from inside the door, and doused the flaming arrow that was stuck in the door jam. Just then, an Indian on horseback caught him dead to rights. Horne turned, wide-eyed, at him, and saw Chief Muatagoci in all his glory. Muatagoci had a fire in his eyes that rivaled that of Grigson when he saw money. Muatagoci raised his rifle and fired, but Horne's experience and anticipation allowed him enough time to roll out of the way, off the porch, and onto the ground. Horne jumped to a standing position and ran straight ahead toward the livery. The door was halfway open and he drove into the crevice, plunging his body between the doors.

Inside the livery, he saw the wagon fully loaded, but did not see Cliven Daniels. Horne had his pistol at the ready, in case of Indians. He searched around for a moment until he was at the rear of the wagon. On the wagon's gate, waiting to be put further in, were some rolled blankets and a couple of half-empty boxes of tack. Among the assorted goods, lying on a oil cloth spread out on the gate, was the prize rifle with carved ivory stock and gold fittings. If that didn't convince Horne that Daniels was not the person he thought him to be, the pistol put to the back of his skull would do just that.

"So, you're our thief?" Horne willed himself to stay calm.

"I prefer opportunist," said Daniels.

"Planning on making a run for it yourself, I see."

"It looks like this town is lost."

"Not if you help us."

"That's not my job, Horne. It's yours."

"What is your job, exactly?"

"Nevermind that." Daniels was impatient. "Now, turn around, slowly, and drop that pistol in the dirt."

Horne did as he was told, and found himself staring into Daniels' pistol barrel. Daniels kicked the marshal's gun beneath the wagon.

"Now, get on your knees and use that rope lying by the wheel to tie yourself up. I don't want you making this hard for me."

"Why not kill me?"

"I don't want you dead."

"I will be if you abandon us now."

"As long as Muatagoci meets his end, my job is done."

"What does that mean?"

Daniels didn't give him an answer. He was already latching the wagon gate up and ascending the wagon wheel onto the buckboard. He grabbed the reins of the two horses fitted to the rig. Without another word, the thief hawed the horses and they shot out the front doors and down the street. Horne easily removed his bindings, which he'd tied loosely on purpose. He grabbed up his pistol and ran to the street. The wagon was heading eastward down Main Street. There was no way to catch him on foot. Meanwhile, the Utes were on the western side near Ms. Fink's, fighting with some townsfolk who had managed to become trapped between buildings. Horne suspected they would not make it out alive.

Just then, his ears caught the sound of horses coming in from the east side of town and turned to see at least two dozen white men on horseback come stampeding down Main Street. The majority of the horsemen blew past Daniels' wagon and continued down the street until they met the Utes, where a firefight ensued.

A black mare stayed behind with the wagon. As Horne approached, he recognized the man holding a gun to Cliven Daniels. It was Deputy Seth Barr.

"Seth!" Marshal Horne yelled out. "How did you...?"

"Once I reached Selby's, I was surprised to find nearly two dozen men already there. They were planning their own raid on Muatagoci and his Utes. Selby and the others agreed with my assumption that we needed to protect Talon's Crossing first and foremost," reported Barr.

"Well, I'm sure glad you were right, Seth," Horne grinned. "I sure wasn't." He glanced at Daniels, who was unarmed.

Before Horne could comment further, Barr motioned down the opposite side of the street, where a shift in the battle had occurred and the braves began fleeing from town. Just as they started ascending the rolling hill a half mile out of town, with the white men giving chase, a company of horsemen appeared on the horizon atop the ridge.

"Now, who do you figure that is?" Horne scratched his chin.

As if to answer him, bugles began blaring in the distance and a troop of U.S. Cavalry came riding down upon the fleeing Utes. The battle was quick and decisive. Muatagoci and his tribe were too few and too tired to defend themselves now. They were harshly dispatched and, moments later, no Ute pony was left with a rider on top.

"Thank God we got that telegram off," said Horne. "Looks like you weren't useless after all, Daniels."

"There was no telegram, Marshal," Barr informed Horne about what he'd found in the telegraph office.

"Well, more reason to thank you that you saw past his treachery." Horne walked up beside Daniels, who peered down at Horne from the buckboard.

"I'd like to think you trained me that way, Marshal," Deputy Seth Barr smiled.

✪✪✪

In the aftermath of the battle, as tired bodies found suitable places to rest and motionless ones were moved to their resting places, the U.S. Cavalry came into town to help out, as they could. Among them was Tom Stratford, who'd helped save Darryl Selby and who'd promised to return with a troop.

"Looks like you made good on that promise," Selby stood next to Marshal Horne.

"You folks are good people, and I was tired of seeing good people die for nothing. It almost got me court martialed, but I convinced my superiors to do the right thing."

"And we thank you for it," said a grateful Marshal Horne. "Plus, you managed to take down Chief Muatagoci."

"Not single-handedly. But I don't think he'll be any trouble for the Emerald Valley anymore."

That night, the folks of Talon's Crossing finally got a much-needed rest from the excitement and terror of the previous days. Horne locked Daniels in the jail to await the arrival of his superior, U.S. Marshal James J. Heatherton. Horne was sure Heatherton would be seeing to it personally that Daniels rotted in prison for putting the town in danger.

Two days later, when Heatherton arrived, however, it was in writing only. The letter, addressed specifically to Horne, ordered the release of Daniels. Apparently, Daniels was acting on behalf of the U.S. Marshal's office in using the town as bait to apprehend Chief Muatagoci. "Any casualties were of no significance to the greater well-being of law and order." Reluctantly, Horne released Daniels, despite his later plea, in writing, that he'd been accused of theft and kidnapping of a duly elected official. Daniels, however, did not make a quiet exit from Talon's Crossing.

In the coming days, Grigson re-opened the shooting competition, much to the chagrin of Marshal Horne, who was ready for a little peace and quiet in town. However, the folks of Talon's Crossing had been eagerly awaiting the finale of the contest.

"Ladies and gentlemen," Grigson's voice boomed. "Today, we finish this competition in remembrance of brave men and women that lost their lives earlier this week in defense of the people and the town they loved." The crowd cheered. "So, without further ado, Lady Nordish will attempt to outshoot Mr. Dan Speedman, who has already made his shot for this round. Anson, will you please reveal the prized rifle we will present to our winner."

Anson turned to the wagon and dropped the rear gate to reveal the Winchester box sitting in the back. Using Grigson's key, he unlocked it and opened it up. Shock overtook his face when he looked into the empty box. Grigson's face went pale, the dread of losing it for a second time too much to handle. He fainted.

A horse bolted across the street. It was Marshal Horne's horse. Atop was Cliven Daniels, with the ivory carved stock of the prize rifle sitting in the leather saddle scabbard. Everyone's eyes followed the mare out of town and across the prairie where the cavalry had massacred the Utes only days prior.

Horne grabbed a rifle from the wagon near Ms. Fink's and lifted it up. In the iron sights, he saw the faint figure of Cliven Daniels bouncing steadily on top of his mare. Daniels was now a public horse thief, an offense punishable by death. No damned U.S. Marshal could stop him now. As Daniels started to ascend the slope of the ridge near a half mile away, a gunshot emanated from behind Gideon Horne. Horne turned, as did everyone else, to see Lady Alice Nordish holding her rifle level with the ground, smoke billowing from the barrel. She lowered the gun and placed it at her heels.

Horne looked back at the figure on the slope. His mare stood grazing rider-less. A slumped figure lay motionless on the ground beside the horse.

"What a shot," hollered someone in the crowd.

Grigson, who'd been helped up by one of his employees, walked slowly up beside her. "Quite," he said, "but unfortunately not at the target for this competition."

"Like hell," Mr. Speedman, stepped forward. "I couldn't make that shot in my dreams. I concede to Lady Nordish."

The crowd of townsfolk went wild with cheers and clapping. Many of them patted Speedman on the back for his actions, and everyone wanted to shake Lady Nordish's hand.

After retrieving his horse, Horne removed the rifle from the scabbard and handed it to Lady Nordish. Despite some protests from her friends, Lady Nordish agreed to put the rifle above the bar at the Nest. Not out of appreciation for Speedman and his friends, but in remembrance of the lives lost the Battle of Talon's Crossing, or so the townsfolk like to refer to it. In the coming days, Horne sent a letter detailing the demise of Cliven Daniels. There was never a response.

THE END

Rush of the Remuda

The dim channels of the Emerald Valley lay still under cover of the starlit sky overhead. The swath of indigo that was smeared across the sky did little to keep the rolling vales hidden. Here and there were a few smatterings of foxtail pines and sierra junipers, but the Emerald Valley was, for the most part, a seemingly endless expanse of fertile grazing land. Cradled by the Jarbidge Mountains, the grazing land was home to mobs of wild horses leftover from the Spanish incursion that spent countless days munching their stomachs full of fresh grass and working to build the next generations. That night, the mob was nowhere to be found.

Although seen in a cleft in the western side of Emerald Valley in the early morning hours, Jasper Dorsey strained his eyes across the plain to spot a sign of the horses. From the back of his Palomino mare, he was leaning forward in the saddle to canvas the entire valley below. He wore a dark cotton shirt and typical ranch hand's vest of cow leather. He had removed his brown slouch to aid in his sightline.

Dorsey worked for Benjamin Webb, the owner of the Slanting W Ranch in the southerly portion of the Emerald Valley. Webb was an old resident of the valley, and Dorsey had caught his eye as a stout ranch hand and even better bronc buster. Dorsey was in his early twenties, but was already on track to become a long-standing member of the Slanting W. Just weeks prior, he had stifled the ferocity of a particularly nasty bronc. The feat earned him the honor of scouting the next batch of "sups," or supplementals.

Horses were not the main livestock roaming the Emerald Valley of Nevada. Years prior, when Ben Webb was still a young man from the East looking to make his claim, the mob of wild stallions and mares was gigantic. Those who chose to stake their claims and let loose cattle were rewarded by an abundant supply of grazing land, beautiful vistas, and agreeable weather. Their curse was the ever-dwindling supply of wild horses. Along with the occasional round-up or Indian grab, the decreased grazing land was a blight on the population. Now, nearly a half century later, the herd was not what it once was.

Dorsey caught wind of a distant, continuous thunder in the distance. He stretched out his neck and slowly took in a panoramic view of the landscape below. Nothing. Only swath and darkness lay out before his straining eyes. His mare's ears twitched slightly, and he knew the herd was near. Mr. Webb would want the location before sun-up so Haney, the Slanting W's foreman, and the team could gear up and bring back the choice dozen before lunch. The horses would need to be corralled, branded, shoed, and finally broken in the days to come.

Throughout the years, Webb and other ranchers in the Emerald Valley took horses here and there, filling their stables and selling which ones they chose. After decades of this, Webb and a neighboring rancher, Ezra Peck, came to a gentleman's agreement. They agreed to supplement their cattle income by taking a dozen wild horses from the herd each year apiece to make ends meet. It was always an unspoken agreement that no rancher would take too many horses, so that the herd's numbers would stay stable and prolong the practice into the foreseeable future. Today was Webb's dozen for the year, and he meant to get the choice of the herd.

Even atop his horse, Dorsey felt the rumble in the earth tremble in his saddle. He smiled, knowing the herd was approaching, even though he couldn't see them yet. He wasn't sure what had spooked them, but something was driving the mass of animals faster and faster in his direction. Dorsey didn't fear a stampede, however, as he was perched on a high knoll in the valley and could see down into the dim cleft from where the herd was travelling. He would see them long before they overturned the sod beneath him. He would be back at the Slanting W with their location within the hour, if he rode as hard as he planned to.

Suddenly, the shaking of the ground became so violent his watch chain jangled against his leather vest and the reins shook in his gloved hands. Dorsey looked around swiftly, assessing the valley below in all directions. His lips parted and he let out a shriek of exclamation. To the rear, a quarter of a mile off and approaching fast was the mob of wild horses moving at a speed he had never seen them move. Dorsey slapped his mare's flank and the horse bolted off the knoll and down into the valley. Within seconds, the herd was upon him. His mare, heavy with tack and rider, struggled to outrun the mob of raging animals.

Deciding that he couldn't outrun them, Dorsey decided to cut them off and skirt the edge of the herd to safety. As his mare turned sharply against the wall of thundering hooves, Dorsey lost track of his position. The darkness had arrived as quickly as the horses, and Dorsey struggled to see his position or his escape route. Where was he? What lay ahead of him? Thoughts flooded his mind and his mare whinnied as she gnawed the bit. A shot rang out in the darkness. Dorsey fell from his saddle and hit the ground with a thud. The remuda scattered around him, but an unawares mare trampled his body, twisting and turning him in the dirt. More horses followed, unaware of what tossed around beneath their galloping legs.

After a moment, the herd was gone, thundering down the cleft of the valley toward safety and new pasture. Miles behind them, a Palomino mare stood stamping and neighing, still anxious and excited from the tumultuous events. Her reins lay swinging below her head, and the saddle was empty. Fifty yards away from her lay the still body of Jasper Dorsey. Clumps of dirt and bits of blood covered his pale skin. His clothes were torn and tattered. His gun belt had been ripped and thrown yards away. On the back of his cotton shirt, a large red stain permeated the material. In the middle, a small hole signaled the entrance of a craven and skillful gunshot.

✪✪✪

"Poor man," said Marshal Gideon Horne, lifting himself from his kneeling position. He was a tall man and stoutly built. He wore blue trousers, a white cotton shirt, and a gray wool vest. The right corner of his black frock was held back by the butt of a nickel plated Colt revolver that sat silent in the holster. On the lapel was a six-sided star in brass that read: "Sheriff — Talon's Crossing."

Horne's face held a sullen expression as he stared down at the disfigured body of Jasper Dorsey. His face was downcast and his lips pursed tightly, studying the scene. Around his lips was a graying goatee, except the chin was clean shaven. After a moment, he grabbed the black Boss of the Plains off his head and wiped his sweating brow with the sleeve of his frock. His hair was darker than his beard, but cropped short the way he preferred it. Manageable and presentable, the way he liked his town.

"From what Webb's men can figure, the herd must have caught him by surprise in the darkness," said Deputy Marshal Seth Barr, a young man about half Horne's age, but double as eager on the job. His body was leaner and more compact, but he was tall and fit for the job. His face was a diamond, his cheekbones jutting out to either side. He wore a mustache of brown hair above his upper lip. He wore a similar uniform, but did not have a frock coat to blanket his figure, preferring a simple green suit jacket.

"Yeah," said Horne, pointing his finger at the body. "But unless those horses can shoot, I'd say the bullet hole in his back is the main cause of death."

Barr bent over and inspected the area on Dorsey's body that Marshal Horne had pointed to. Sure enough, and much to Barr's continued reverence for Horne, there was a small hole in the back of Dorsey's shirt and dried blood surrounding it. Barr lifted himself up and put his hands on his hips. As he did, a Colt Bisby appeared from behind his jacket.

"So we've got a murder on our hands and no suspect in sight, beyond a herd of wild ponies off in the valley." Barr spit into the grass. He was chewing a plug of tobacco.

"I'd say the Slanting W is a good a place to start asking questions," Horne said, turning swiftly to leave.

Barr followed after a moment, and the duo passed Johns, the undertaker of Talon's Crossing. The bent old man was dragging a stubborn mule by the reins that pulled behind it a long, empty cart. This would be Jasper Dorsey's temporary purgatory until he could find a spot suitable for his frame in Talon's Crossing Cemetery.

Horne and Barr saddled up their ponies and headed south into the Emerald Valley toward the Slanting W Ranch, home of Ben Webb's outfit. They passed Six-Mile River, a now-five mile tributary from the Jarbidge that suffered a drought some years ago which left a mile in dust. Soon, stray and half-starved cattle appeared and soon thereafter the main herd was upon them. All Angus beef and prime in every way. The fertile grass of Emerald Valley was legendary as cattle sustenance. Webb and Peck were the only two cattleman left in the region and, as such, their cattle were among the choicest beef that entered the cafes and steakhouses of Salt Lake and Boise.

The ranch house soon appeared over the horizon, a large beacon of civilization among the rolling, wild hills. As Horne and Barr approached, the stables, tack houses, and hand quarters swelled from the ground like they had been there all along. The fencing of the corrals separated the bluebird sky into perfect squares and gave an orderly aura to the otherwise hard and non varied landscape. Horne tapped his boot heel on his stallion's ribs and the horse stepped up his pace as they approached the main gates of the Slanting W.

From the corral a mounted rider on a gray stallion rushed toward the lawmen as they approached the ranch house. The gray neighed as it was pulled to a halt, the animal's hooves shoving into the dirt. On top of the beast was a thickly-built man with a square jaw and thick patch of beard.

His face was stern, and its resting position gave an air of anger. On his hip was a thick Colt Single Action Army and in his hand was a Winchester rifle. He looked ready for a war.

"You better find the filthy bastards that did that to Jasper!" shouted the man, his horse moving under the anxious rein work of the rider.

Marshal Horne sat silent in the saddle, obviously a skilled practitioner in the art of listening. He knew Webb and his men would be roaring for a fight with whomever they set their sights on first, whether or not it was the guilty party. Deputy Barr was looking over at Horne, waiting for a response.

"Well," grizzled rider continued. "What the hell are you doin'? You got any suspects, yet?"

"We've got a dead, trampled body of a young man and a short list of people who even knew him," said Horne, "so we'll let you know when it's your turn for questioning."

The man glared back at Marshal Horne. "Are you serious, Marshal? You think I had something to do with this? You are as crackbrained as they say."

Deputy Barr spoke up. "Marshal Horn is one of the best…"

Horne put his hand up in an effort to quell Barr's words. The obedient deputy stopped immediately, but his lips writhed in frustration.

"Just don't go far, is what I'm saying," Horne added.

The man wheeled his pony around, "Oh, you'll be seein' me, and so will that dirty coward Peck and his no-good foreman Cooley. They'll all be seein' me." He turned the horse and bolted across the ranch toward the corral.

When he was gone, Barr said, "I don't like that fellah."

Horne nudged his pony onward toward the house. "He's the foreman of the Slanting W, Micah Haney. Been here a long time. Hands, let alone good ones, are hard to come by."

"That don't give him the right to go mouthin' off at you, Marshal, let alone threatening Peck and his men."

The two men reached the hitching post of the house and dismounted. They tied their reins tightly and walked up the wooden steps. The home was grand, but not special. It was large, one of the largest in the area, and was well-built over many years with strong, oak timber from the Emerald Valley. Webb and his wife had made their family here, built their business, and created an empire from the porch Horne and Barr were standing on. Webb could have afforded a more luxurious abode, but the weathered timber was a symbol of his ability to last longer than most in such unforgiving country. He liked it to show.

As he knocked on the door, Horne replied to Barr's previous comment. "I agree. It don't give him the right, but you can't blame him. If what he said was true about Peck being involved, we might have a range war on our hands. Best to get the facts before we make any assumptions."

A bright faced girl answered the door. She was pretty, with long brunette curls hanging down her back. Her neck was thin, but only because of her stature and not her breeding. She wore a plain, blue dress, with a white sash tied around her waist. She smiled when she saw the lawman's badges pinned to the men's coats. She bit her lip in nervous agitation.

"Marshal, Deputy, come in, please."

"Thank you, Ellie," Marshal Horne removed his hat as he entered.

Inside the main foyer of the home was a large stone fireplace. Atop the mantle was an old flintlock musket, likely belonging to Webb's father or grandfather. The gun was well-polished, but did not look recently fired. Horne had come to assess such minute detail in nearly twenty years as a lawman. No detail went unnoticed to his trained eye. Ellie Webb walked them to the sitting area and then left. Seth Barr's eyes followed her out of the room, clearly enamored by her beauty. Horne was uninterested, looking at the old man who had entered the room from the office to the left.

Ben Webb stopped when he saw Marshal Horne. His face was weathered and wrinkled from many days in the saddle, and his hair was white and neatly combed. The recent years had given rise to a gentry element in his style, and the old man had taken to caring more for his appearance. That and his inability to ride a horse. The year prior, he was thrown from his horse and trampled, leaving him unable to walk or ride. Webb sat in a wheeled chair, staring at Horne.

Horne fiddled with his hat in his hands. "I'm sorry for your loss, Ben. From what I've heard, Dorsey was a good hand."

"My best," Webb said in his deep baritone voice. "Dorsey was a damned fine horseman and bronc buster. He would have been foreman if it wasn't for Haney's experience."

Horne pursed his lips, studying the situation. He couldn't predict Webb's next words. "So... any idea how this happened to such a skilled horseman?"

"Only one way," Webb deduced. "Goddamned Peck and his gunslingers."

"How d'you figure that?" Horne's eyebrows crinkled into a questioning look.

Webb used his strong arms to move the wheels on the chair. He moved the chair closer to Horne, then glared up at him through piercing blue eyes.

"For God knows how long, we've had unspoken terms about the wild horses that roam the valley. We each get our pick of a dozen each spring. No questions asked. It helps supplement the income, especially after a hard winter. Plus, those wild stallions run like hell. Over the past few years, I noticed more and more horses disappearing from the herd. I always take my dozen, and no more!" Webb held up a stern finger skyward.

"What makes you think Peck's to blame?"

"Who else? The Slanting W and the Tipped E are the only ones left who even care for them horses. Besides, that herd is a daily sight. We'd know if some stranger was stealing from 'em."

"So if it ain't you, then Peck is the answer, huh? What if it's one of the hands supplementing his own pay?" Horne suggested.

"Not one of mine, dammit!" Webb shouted, visibly upset by the mention of one of his men.

"Could be one of Peck's?"

The comment cooled Webb's anger. The old man sat back in his chair, sighing. "Yeah, maybe, I don't know. It ain't me or mine, I know that. If Peck's man is at fault, he needs to be strung up!"

"Just remember, Ben," cautioned Horne, "those horses are free game. Your agreement is a gentleman's. Most folks don't think that way anymore."

Webb leaned forward, ready to bite.

"I'm not saying it's right, them taking from the herd. All I'm worried about is finding out why and what led to the death of Jasper Dorsey this morning," Horne concluded. He turned away from Webb. "I'm heading back into Talon's Crossing to review the case so far. I'll keep you informed."

With that, Horne and Barr walked out of the foyer and through the front door, placing their hats on their heads as they did. Webb did not move or respond, but seemed to be stewing over the day's events. As Horne and Barr mounted their horses, Ellie came running from the side of the house opposite the corral, where Haney and his men were gearing up to go round up this year's batch of horses. She looked nervous, like before.

"Marshal," she said almost in a whisper.

Horne looked down at her, tipping the end of his hat as he did. Barr did the same.

"I don't know what my father told you, but...Oh, I don't know!"

"What is it, Miss Webb?" Horne leaned on his saddle horn.

"Daddy has been taking more horses than he's supposed to. But so has Mr. Peck. They've been at it for a couple years now, back and forth. One takes twenty, one takes twenty five. It's a competition to them, now." Ellie wiped sweat from her brow.

"And you think Jasper Dorsey is caught up in it? A bystander caught in the crossfire?" .

"Yes— I don't know," she was confused. "All I know is I want both ranches to continue in peace. We've always had good relations till the last few years. Now, we don't even visit anymore."

"Well, thank you for that, Miss Ellie." Horne tipped his hat.

The girl backed away from the mare and allowed the lawmen to ride away. Horne and Barr kicked their mounts into a run and took off down the trail. She continued watching as they faded into the horizon, down into the Emerald Valley and toward Talon's Crossing. When their image became faded and no longer discernible from the distant foxtail pines, she turned and disappeared into the house.

✪✪✪

The town of Talon's Crossing sat in a flat in the heart of Emerald Valley. Nearly fifty years prior, Henry Talon led a wagon train of settlers west from St. Louis. The group passed through the Emerald Valley on their way to California and gold, and fell in love with the area. Talon became the town's first mayor and was the owner/proprietor of the longest running saloon in town: the Eagle's Nest.

The Eagle's Nest, or Nest, as most townsfolk called it, was the centerpiece of town. A large wooden sculpture of an eagle, wings spread, sat atop the otherwise bland building. Beside it, on one side of Main Street, was the taller Plains Hotel, the First Bank of Emerald Valley, and Peabody's Livery & Corral. Various other buildings lined the street further, but many were constantly changing brands and owners. The other side of town held the Marshal's Office & Jail, various blacksmiths and tack related enterprises, a few other saloons and restaurants, and a slew of mercantiles and shops.

As Marshal Horne and Deputy Barr walked their horses up to the Marshal's Office, they noticed a man sitting on the edge of the porch, holding a bloody bandana to his mouth. He wore the typical garb of a ranch cowboy: dirty jeans, a fresh cotton shirt, a vest, and a crinkled weather-beaten hat. He wore a Colt Peacemaker on his hip, crossdraw. When he saw Horne and Barr, he stood from the porch and lowered the bandana. He had an uncommonly handsome face, clean shaven and of a consistent pigment. Although he could pass for any country gentlemen, on this day, he looked like he had been dipped, swished, and hung out to dry. His nose was visibly broken, twisted to an awkward angle, and his lips and cheeks were cut and bruised. Someone, or a few someones, had beaten him good.

Marshal Horne dismounted and hitched his mount. He looked up to the porch at the young man standing opposite him. He recognized the man, but had a hard time recalling his name. It was obvious this fellah wasn't a town dweller like most folks Horne knew. Horne could probably place a man from counties over, but names were another thing altogether. So many variations, constantly changing, and a curse to an uneducated man like himself. Reading anything other than the paper was beyond him, but he was educated in the school of the hills and plains. That was all that had mattered so far into his career.

"I know you, son," Horne nodded. "You ride with Ezra Peck and the Tipped E?"

The young man puffed out his chest. "Yes, sir. Name's Travis Cooley, and I'm the foreman for Mr. Peck."

"I see," Horne walked past Cooley into his office.

Inside Horne hung his hat on the rack at the door and placed his rifle on the gun rack. There were four cells on the right side of the office, but all were empty. Horne preferred it that way. Men in cells tended to try to be men out of cells. If they were innocent or guilty, he wanted the trial done and over with as quickly as possible. Less stress that way. Horne took a seat behind the large, wooden desk in the center of the office. Papers covered the desk from the months prior, and a small stack of wanted posters and telegrams were neatly piled in the corner.

Cooley and Deputy Barr walked in the front door as Horne sat down. Barr began to put up his things and Cooley took a position in front of Horne's desk, still rubbing his jaw and broken nose. Horne expected Cooley to rush into a tangent, blaming someone for his broken nose or bringing up the horses. But he didn't. Cooley stood there, living up to his name and staring hard at Marshal Horne.

Horne lifted his head, put his arms on his desk, and bit, "So? What happened?"

"Micah Haney… and his goons."

"Haney?" Barr chimed in from across the office. "We just left him."

"Yeah, well, his men roughed me up real good on the trail east of town. They made it pretty clear Haney was sending a message."

"What message is that? Anything to do with those horses?" Asked Horne.

"It's no secret Mr. Peck and Webb have been at it the last few years," Cooley replied. "But we haven't done a damn thing to those horses that wasn't right in line with the agreement they made years back."

"That's what I'm getting from both sides."

"It's God's honest truth, Marshal," Cooley swore.

Horne inspected Cooley's face. He couldn't tell the portion of truth that he held in his brow or his eyes. It was clear, however, that Cooley believed the words he was saying. Horne knew he had to bring in Haney to get his side of his whole ordeal. Plus, he was interested to know what Haney was up to in the wake of Jasper Dorsey's death. Haney was the type of person who reacted strongly, good or bad, no matter the situation, and Horne knew this. It would take a firm hand to hold him back from retaliating and starting a full scale range war.

"All right," Horne tugged his chin. "I'll bring in Haney to get his side. If he confesses, he'll be jailed and fined. If not, well, he'll get due process."

"Thank you, Marshal," Cooley nodded and left the office.

Horne turned to Barr. "Seth, I need you to go back out the Slanting W and bring in Micah Haney."

❂❂❂

Micah Haney sat stern-faced across the desk from Marshal Horne. His lips were hidden by his beard, but they were likely pulled tightly together in a frown. They had been arguing.

"I told you, I don't know who did the beatin', but it wasn't me," Haney professed, crossing his arms.

"So you're telling me a foreman of the largest ranch in the Emerald Valley doesn't know where his men come and go?" asked the Marshal.

"I'm a foreman, not a father."

"And a hell of a pain to get anything out of," Horne snapped. It was a rare moment when Marshal Horne used profanity. He was not a regular churchgoer, nor a particularly Biblical man, but he saw profanity as the absence of a more intelligent thought. As such, he used it sparingly.

"I can't give you anything if I don't know anything."

"At least give me the names of the men and we'll be done here. I've got too many facts to go over to waste my time arguing."

Haney rose from his chair and walked over to Deputy Barr's desk. He scribbled on a notepad with a pencil and then put his hat on his head.

"Marshal, those Peck sonsabitches got something coming for what they've done to Jasper, but I would make damn sure I finish the job when

"It's the God's honest truth, Marshal,"

I do it." Haney slammed the door behind him as he left.

Marshal Horne put his head in his hands. It was an unusually difficult day, and he had not experienced one in some time. He sighed, then sucked in a deep breath, content to make the best of the rest of the sunlight he had. As he grabbed for a piece of paper, the office door creaked open again. Horne cursed underneath his breath. He looked up to see Ellie Webb standing in the doorway. Horne quickly rose to his feet.

"Miss Barr," Horne greeted, adjusting his shirt.

"Marshal," she smiled at both men. "Deputy."

"How can we help you?" Barr sat up straight.

"I...well...I...Oh, Lord, I just can't stand it no more." She walked over to an empty chair and sat down. Horne quickly tried to adjust it for her.

"What is it, Miss Webb?" he asked.

"Those... men. They've all got fire in their bellies over these horses." Her face was flushed with red.

"I know it can be tough, ma'am, but things like this tend to get blown out of proportion. Someone takes an extra horse, then the next takes ten, and so on."

"But when does it end, Marshal?"

Horne hesitated to tell her it never did, unless it ended with someone lying dead on the prairie. Instead, he lowered his head and sighed.

"It ends when both sides see that what they got is better than what they could have in a hundred years," he answered finally.

Ellie burst into tears. Horne had not expected this and was visibly confused. He turned to look at Barr, whose wide eyes told a similar tale. After she sobbed for a moment, she looked up, eyes full of tears.

"I'm the cause of all this hatred, Marshal," she blurted between sobs.

"No, no, no." Horne took a seat next to her.

"Yes, sir, I am. I've been steady with Travis Cooley for a year or so now. We plan to get married as soon as he asks Daddy. But with Haney, and now this horse business, I don't see how that's ever gonna happen now."

"I'm sorry to hear that, Miss Ellie. But how does Haney figure in?"

"He's been a hand since I was a girl, ten years or so and when Travis and me started courtin' he made it clear he had eyes for me. Obviously, Travis didn't take kindly to that, so they had a tumble a few months back and today Travis comes in bloody and beaten. Oh..."

It made sense now, thought Horne. Haney wasn't upset about the horses, but about Ellie and Cooley. The horses were an old man's feud, but the eye of a beautiful woman was a young man's game. Horne quickly decided to bring in both men to settle this once and for all. His one thought, however, was how Jasper Dorsey's death figured into this mess. Another thought for another time.

Barr escorted Ellie out of the office and onto her mare. Horne called out for Barr from his desk, telling him to ride east where he still might catch Haney on the trail. Horne was going to fetch Travis Cooley from Peck's place. As Horne grabbed his rifle off the rack and readied himself to ride, Barr came rushing in the door.

"Marshal! There's a fight at the Nest. It's Haney and Cooley!"

Horne and Barr rushed across Main Street to the Eagle's Nest. The fight had already spilled out of the front doors and into the street. A crowd of cheering men was surrounding the action on the inside. As Horne approached, he saw Haney, the larger of the two, wail into Cooley with a stiff right uppercut. The punch sent Cooley reeling backward into the raised porch of the Nest.

As Cooley went to retaliate, Barr lunged in between the two and tackled Cooley back against the porch. Haney seized the opportunity and tried to attack Cooley as he was subdued. Horne, too old for a fistfight, pulled his pistol, flipped it, and cracked the butt on Haney's skull. The big man fell to the ground and the crowd of men fell silent.

"All right!" Horne shouted. "Clear out. This mess's over."

Horne directed Barr to get their horses from the hitching post outside the Nest. A moment later, Horne and Barr loaded Haney's limp body over the saddle and patted the horse toward the jail. Horne grabbed Cooley, who was waiting his turn on the porch, and led him after the horse. At the jail, Horne placed Cooley inside one cell, while Barr dragged Haney's limp body to the other.

"Luckily we had two cells, huh, Marshal?" Barr grinned, wiping the sweat off his face.

"Long as there ain't no more to put in there."

The door to the office opened and in walked a pretty sight. Horne turned and gruffed.

"Looks like our problems are just beginning," he mumbled under his breath.

It was Ellie Webb again. Her brunette curls dangled low on her shoulders, as her head was slung over, her chin nearly touching her chest. As Barr continued putting away the inmates, Horne walked toward Ellie. When she heard him, she lifted her head and sniffled back her emotion. Horne could tell she had been crying.

"Miss Ellie, please. This isn't helping."

Horne stopped a few feet from her and waited for her response, but it was a hard sell for her. She sniffled back her emotion again, lightly touching her nose with the tip of her hand.

"I...oh!" she began weeping again.

Horne thought of grabbing her, but he knew it was not the proper thing. Although Horne was not a rock, he did respect the rules of his time. He had found, despite years of breaking those rules, that these little things had meaning. In the least, he would respect these things when he could. When he could no longer, well, that was another story.

"It's all my fault, Marshal," Ellie took up her familiar lament again.

"What in blazes do you mean? What's your fault?" Horne's patience was near the end of the trail. His gruff exasperated look penetrated her wall of tears.

"Them boys being locked up, the fighting, the arguments..." Her voice faded away.

Horne lightly touched her shoulders and led her to a chair on the opposite side of his desk. When she sat, Horne leaned back against the desk for balance.

"Explain," Horne prompted. "This time...all of it."

"You see, Micah has had eyes for me for years now. I guess it's natural, him being so close to me so long, but I think of him more as a cousin than a suitor."

"And what's the problem? Why the fighting?"

"Well... you see, Travis and I... we..." She trailed off again.

Ellie didn't have to finish for Horne to comprehend. Young love was at play. A triangle of death for anyone in it or around it. Micah, the man who saw her grow into a beautiful young woman, and Travis, the boy across the Valley, to whom her love was as fleeting as the clouds. Although Horne's wife, Amanda, had died in childbirth quite a few years ago, Horne pitied them. He remembered the feeling, the passions. It was a damn tough thing to avoid, especially at their age.

"So... them fighting, it's over you, for you?"

Ellie nodded.

"Nothing else?"

Now she looked at Horne confused. "Isn't that enough? I don't understand."

God, to be so young and naïve. Horne took pity on her.

"Well, I guess we'll let them settle down a bit and set 'em free. No use faulting men for being men."

Just then the door to the jail burst open. In the doorway stood a young man with the faint outlining of a beard. His hair was long, blonde, and scraggly. His features were catlike, and his hands were outstretched like he was searching for something in a dark room. Behind Horne, Travis Cooley pulled himself against the steel bars of the cell he was in. Once he caught sight of the man at the door, he yelled out "Charlie?"

Horne had moved his hand to the iron on his gun belt, but then turned and asked Cooley, "You know him?"

"Yeah, he works for the Tipped E. Charlie Toler."

"Sorry to bust in like this, Marshal, but we got a big problem," Charlie's words were quick, and he was out of breath by the end of the sentence. Horne could tell he'd been riding straight from the Tipped E.

"Spill it, then, son."

"One of our men—James Prichard—he's been kilt. Run over by a slew of horses in the Valley out past the Slanting W."

"Sorry to hear it, really am, but how do you figure it's a matter for the law?"

"Well…" Charlie stammered. "We figured it's one of them Webb boys' done it."

"So a man is stampeded and it's a murder? What is it with this town? Those kind of things happen," Barr stood next to Horne.

"Yeah?" Cooley spoke through the bars of his cell. "But two men in one day? Seems fishy to me."

"Yeah it sure does," Haney said from the adjacent cell. "We both know you had a hand in Jasper's death. Mr. Webb did the right thing and got some payback."

"I didn't have nothing to do…" Cooley retorted. Horne came over and quieted the both of 'em with a shout.

"We won't argue like this in front of a lady. Haney, you say payback. Am I supposed to believe Ben Webb sent his men to have this man—Prichard—killed?"

"Well, I don't know for sure, but, if it was me running the W, I woulda done it."

"Then I'm glad you don't," Ellie said, rising from her chair. "Micah, I'm sad to hear you talk like this, about killing men who ain't done nothing wrong. And Travis, I'm sad to see you sitting in that cell. And Marshal, I'm… you… I'm just sorry."

Ellie grabbed her hat from the chair and stormed off through the front door. Charlie sidestepped as she marched by.

"I swear to God, Haney, if you and the W had something to do with Jimmy Prichard's death, I'll kill you dead," promised Cooley, speaking through his teeth.

"Enough!" Horne ordered loudly. For a moment, he and the others in the room were content in the silence. For Haney and Cooley, it gave them more time to hate one another. For Charlie, it gave him time to rest. And for Seth Barr, the loyal deputy, it gave him time to learn.

Horne contemplated the goings on. Two murders in one day in the same method? He had heard of coincidences, but the odds were pretty far fetched. Yet, Horne wasn't even sure the second death was even murder. Men who lived with horses often died by horses. No man could calm the rush of the remuda when it got going. The most skilled or experienced cowhand was but a speck in the might of a herd of wild horses that didn't want to be caught. Horne wasn't sure what was up, but he knew where he had to go. He grabbed his rifle off the gun rack as he walked by and then his hat off the rack at the door. He started past Charlie, then stopped, and looked back.

"Seth, I'm going out to the Tipped E with Charlie here. I got some questions need answered. Stay here, make sure these two don't talk unless it's to God or their momma, not that either would want anything to do with what they have to say."

With that, Horne motioned to Charlie and they saddled up out front, kicked their horses, and disappeared into the Valley toward the Tipped E.

✪✪✪

By the time Horne and Charlie caught sight of the Tipped E Ranch in the distance, it was only by the lights that penetrated the darkness from inside the house. The Tipped E sat directly west of the Slanting W, and for what it lacked in fertile soil it made up for in flat land and water sources. Ezra Peck hosted the annual Fall Festival on the north side of his property toward Talon's Crossing. Everyone knew Peck, and most liked him or didn't mind his presence, but that reputation was wearing thin over the past few years. The ongoing feud with Webb mixed with some underhanded business dealings in town had made the Tipped E a shell of its former glory. Some dissenters even went so far as to host a rival Fall Festival the year prior.

A number of horses were locked up in the corral, and as they passed, Horne caught sight of two armed men standing watch over them in the darkness. At the front of the home of Ezra Peck, Charlie dismounted and took Horne's pony from him to get her hitched and watered. Horne wasted no time ascending the stairs on the home and knocking firmly on the door. He was getting plain tired of the pleasantries. He was getting tired, in general.

Ezra Peck opened the door. He was a small man, but round and thick. While his belly had expanded in his old age, you could still tell his figure boasted quite a few muscles from a life of hard labor. Peck was a top trail boss on the cattle drives of yesteryear, and he had the confidence of one, too. His face was red and sagging, with lines from many-a-day in the saddle and fields. He had no facial hair, but a thick lock of flat white hair that came out from underneath his hat. He was dressed in full hunting regalia, from his buckskin breeches to the leather shot bag on his waist.

"Planning on doing some hunting, Ezra?" Horne stepped through the front door.

"If those sonsabitches come after me again, you God-damned right I am," said Peck. Horne instantly remembered his filthy mouth and shook his head at the immature sound of its movements.

As Horne entered the living room, he caught sight of Peck's two sons: Adam and Abel. They were strong, middle-aged men and Horne knew they both had families of their own. It was unlikely they supported their father's ongoing feud with Webb, as it tarnished the reputation of the ranch and land they would inherit in the coming years. Both sons sat on the chairs that faced him. The old man kept pacing around the room.

"And if they try to get us in the night, I've got some surprises for them, I tell you!" Peck warned, holding up his rifle.

"Now hold on, Ezra, no need to go gunslinging around," Horne cautioned. "I got questions need answered before some more death is on our hands."

Ezra gave a disinterested grunt and stared out the window.

"Ezra, listen, both you and Webb got a man lying dead in a coffin at the moment. It's no time to start filling any more. We need to figure out what's going on here."

"I'll tell you what's going on…" began Adam, the older of the two sons.

His father quickly turned to his son, "Quiet down, boy!"

Adam shut his mouth and leaned back in his chair.

"I'll tell you what's going on," Ezra yelled. "That goddamned Ben Webb is trying to steal *my* horses! We had a deal, and he broke it."

"I know, Ben told me that…"

"Oh! I see, Marshal, you've been convoluting with Webb. Now you come to see if I incriminate myself before you haul me off to jail."

"No, I…" Horne couldn't get in a single word.

"And then you gonna take my land and my grandchildren'll be picking sticks off the prairie while the Webbs live high off my hogs!" Spittle flew from Peck's mouth.

Horne shouted to quiet Peck, as he had done in the jail an hour beforehand. Although Horne did not curse, nor yell at folks, his shout was that of a disappointed father. In it, Peck recognized his own father, and stopped speaking. Adam and Abel Peck both held back grins in their chairs.

"I won't have you and Webb spinning a tale of conspiracy in my territory," Horne declared. "I'm here for answers, same as with Webb. If you give me straight answers, we might be one step closer to solving this thing."

Peck did not reply.

"Who found Prichard?"

Peck did not reply. He was staring at a portrait above the fireplace that depicted a herd of stallions crossing the plains.

Adam spoke up in his father's place. "Kent Stephenson, a cowhand."

"What was Prichard doing out near the Tipping W?" Horne continued.

The Peck boys gave matching glances to one another.

Adam spoke again. "Well, Marshal, to be brutally honest, he was scoutin' the Tipping W, after what happened earlier."

"For what?"

Abel jumped in. "Just to keep an eye on 'em all."

There was silence. With his hands on his hips, Horne stared at Abel. Uncomfortable with the staring match, Abel writhed in his chair moving from side to side. Finally, he looked at his elder brother and dropped his head.

"We was planning to steal the horses they got earlier today."

Horne thought for a moment. "Well, that don't make you the murderers, much less thieves."

"What?" Abel was clearly puzzled. "But we was planning to steal 'em. Daddy didn't know, but we knew what we was doing. If we gotta pay for it, we will."

"No, son," Horne shook his head. "Thinking a thing don't make you a thief, just like wanting to kill someone don't make you a killer. What made you two think to steal 'em?"

"Haney gave us the inside track," answered Adam.

"Haney? Micah Haney, foreman of the Tipping W?"

"Yes sir. Said they had a herd of ponies coming in just before daybreak and they were asking half the usual price for 'em."

"We figured it was a gesture," Abel explained. "You know, of good faith, with the feud and all. It wasn't till Charlie rode back from town this morning that we heard one of their boys got killed bringing 'em in. After that we sent Jimmy, that's Jimmy Prichard, out to check on the horses we wanted. Hadn't heard anything in hours, 'til Kent—who was out riding— showed up with Jimmy's body in tow."

"Yeah," Adam confirmed. "And we're still not sure exactly why Haney was on about selling them horses so cheap."

Horne thought just how complicated everything had become. What started as a stampede accident turned into a range war, then a love triangle, and now a side deal gone bad. What did everything have in common?

"I know why," said Ezra Peck, who had been staring at the painting this entire time. He turned and looked at his sons, then at Horne.

"Caleb Haney wants the Tipping W for himself," the old man revealed.

"What?" Horne and the Peck boys gasped in unison.

"Ain't nothing been the same in this Valley since Webb lost his legs two years back. It made Webb bitter, and soured our previously happy arrangement."

"What's that got to do with Haney?" Marshal Horne scratched his head.

"Haney's the one who crippled ole' Webb."

"How do you figure?"

"I was there when it happened, Marshal. We were out scouting the herd like we used to do every spring. See what stallions we want, what we don't want, and divide everything up. Cooley and Haney were there, and a few other men. After a while, Webb and Haney disappeared, and we all set out to find 'em before a big storm rolled in on the Valley. I came upon 'em both talking in a ravine, watering their horses. I called out to 'em but they couldn't hear me. I watched a while, then caught sight of something I thought was mighty odd. While Webb was gettin' a drink from the stream, Haney loosened the front cinch of Webb's saddle. In rolled the storm, with thunder and lighting, and sure enough that herd of horses came rolling right down into that ravine for safety. It wasn't nothing for two men to get outta there in time, but Webb's saddle came undone and he fell off his horse and got trampled. Haney made it out and didn't return for hours, until the storm left. Claimed he was out looking for Webb."

"And you held onto this information for two years?"

"Do you know what it's like to hold a secret like that? It's killed me. On one hand, Webb turned sour and ain't been much of a neighbor since that day, plus knowing his right-hand-man is the one who done it?" Peck hesitated. "That's like holding a lit stick of dynamite.'

Horne did not respond. Peck was right. This wasn't information you threw around willy-nilly. Especially with land and money at stake, this could potentially send a man to his death. Now that he knew, Horne had to act on it. Haney was already incarcerated, so that was half done. Only thing left to do was take Peck's statement, get the charges to Judge Rayburn in Battle Mountain, and then find a way to tell Ben Webb. No doubt Webb would want Haney's life after that."

"Leaves one question unanswered," Horne directed toward Peck. "Why would he do it?"

"Why wouldn't he? Everyone knows he's like a son to Webb. With the old man dead and gone, the Slanting W is ripe for the taking."

"Yeah. And so is the hand of his only daughter."

"If he married the girl, he'd have every legal right to take the Slanting W."

The front door of the house opened and someone ran through the foyer into the living room. It was Charlie Toler. He looked like he was in a rush again.

"Boss, there's a man out here, says he's got news for the Marshal"

"Well, let him in," Peck waved his hand.

"He won't, says he's got to get back to town, right quick."

Horne and the Peck family followed Charlie out of the house. Outside, Johns was sitting on the top of a cart. The mule that was tied up in the traces was breathing heavily, its pink tongue lolled. Johns was the undertaker of Talon's Crossing. He looked angry.

"Marshal," Johns saluted.

"Johns, what the hell is going on?"

"Marshal, I gotta a big quota 'bout to be filled in town." Johns used his thumb to point back north toward Talon's Crossing.

"What'd you mean?"

"Haney and Cooley, they've gotten themselves into a gunfight."

"What? How? They were in the jail last I left 'em?"

"Not sure, but they ain't in there, anymore."

Horne was speechless. It was one thing to break out of the jail, another to start a gunfight in the middle of his town. But to take out his deputy? To a marshal, especially to one as righteous as Gideon Horne, this was too far.

Johns continued. "They got a couple o' guns and now they're shootin'. That poor Webb girl is caught down in the middle, too."

"Ellie Webb? How'd that happen?"

"Not sure, I just dig graves."

"Fair enough," Horne accepted the man's neutrality in such matters. Johns buried everyone equal. "All right, let's light out. I'm sure Webb'll be there once he finds out Ellie is gone from the Slanting W. Ezra, you and your boys better come with us to get Cooley calmed down."

Horne mounted his horse alongside Charlie and let out after Johns and his cart, which was already heading past the corral. Peck and his boys followed in behind them and they all lit out toward town. Soon, they disappeared from sight in the darkness of the Emerald Valley, the white moon high overhead.

As the group approached Talon's Crossing some time later, the town was still a shining beacon among the sea of darkness surrounding it. Main Street was lit by makeshift oil lamps donated by the Mayor, Myles Wallace, the previous year. As they got within earshot, the gunfire erupting inside the town limits became apparent.

"Gentlemen, I'd appreciate it if you hold back a ways and let me and Ezra head in to diffuse the situation," Marshal Horne directed his oration toward the Peck boys and Johns.

No one argued, so Horne and Peck headed out together down Main Street. While the gunfire was sparse, and sounded like only the shooting of two men, it was more action than Talon Crossing had seen since the Ute Indian raids the previous year. Horne was born in the Emerald Valley, and had resided there all his life. Even the War Between the States had not pulled him from his home.

"All right, Ezra, once we get closer, hang back a bit and I'll go in and see what's going on. Neither Haney nor Cooley got qualms with me. Can't say the same for you."

"Got it, but I'll be ready," Peck tapped his rifle against his chest.

Horne dismounted, pulled his pistol, and started walking toward the center of town, near the jail. He kept a wary eye open in the darkness, scanning every darkened crevice in the shadowy town. Horne led with his pistol, his shadow dancing on the livery stable wall to his left, and some horses in the corral sniffed at him. A shot rang out in the street ahead and Horne ducked down momentarily. Another shot rang out, and Horne raised his head a little to assess the scene.

Someone was crouched down behind a wagon that had unluckily parked out in front of the Nest. Across the street was the Marshal's Office and Jail, where someone's shadow appeared every minute or so in the candlelight from inside. Whoever broke them out was not visible. "Damn,"

"They got a couple o' guns and now they're shootin'."

whispered Horne to himself. He knew there was no good way to go about this. He had to pick a side, take them out in secret. Or, go right down the middle.

Horne remembered a line his former boss, Marshal Zane Pollard, had told me when he was just a deputy: "A lawman often finds himself in the middle of what is right and what is the law. If you should ever find yourself in such a place, the only way out is *through*."

Horne hadn't really considered, nor understood, the sentiment until now. He thought of Seth Barr, injured and potentially dead, lying somewhere in the dirt, or in the jail. He got angry, and such an emotion did not sit well on Gideon Horne. He had a temper as a young man, the fire quelled by the hotter fire of passionate love for a woman. Since her death, Horne had stifled the flame, but now it reared its head again. He remembered the last man he had shot: Lou Holbert. A drunk, but good with a gun. Holbert lay cold and dead in the Talon's Crossing Cemetery. "Johns better get a few more graves ready," Horne said aloud.

He lifted himself up and walked on, down the center of Main Street, straight between the Marshal's Office and the Nest. The shadow in the window of the Marshal's Office appeared again, and Horne pointed his gun at it. No gunfire came pouring through the broken glass window, so Horne turned back to the roadway and continued on. Suddenly, another shadow appeared to his left, this time from the front window of the Nest. Again, no gunfire erupted.

"Haney! Cooley!" Shouted Horne.

No reply.

"You both have run my town amuck, and now I aim to deal with you," Horne continued. "In any way I have to."

Suddenly, the shadow in the Marshal's Office window disappeared. A few seconds passed, and then Travis Cooley appeared in the doorway. He was armed, but his pistol was not pointed. Horne pointed his pistol at Cooley, just in case.

"Sorry Marshal. But Micah Haney has his due comin'."

"I'll deal with that."

"But Marshal, your man lay shot in the leg in one of the cells, just like the man who lay dead from my outfit."

The thought of Seth lying bleeding in a cell gave Horne chills.

"How'd you two get out?" Horne kept a watchful eye on the shadow in the Nest window.

"I was sleeping when I heard a commotion. Your man had tried to check on Haney, when Haney jumped him and shot him. Tried to shoot me dead in my cell, till Ellie came burstin' through the door and shot Haney to save me."

"Ellie? God, is she okay?"

"She's right here, Marshal," Cooley pointed to his left. After a second, Ellie's head appeared in the doorway. She did not look happy.

"I'm sorry…Marshal Horne, but I couldn't let him kill Travis. I love him!"

"It's all right, Ellie," Horne said softly. "I understand. Now, let's all drop the guns and…" Horne froze. He noticed the shadow in the Nest window had disappeared. He looked around, judging the scene in front of him. Nothing.

Travis Cooley looked down upon Ellie Webb, who stared up at him from the floor of the Marshal's Office. He stared into her eyes, longingly, and saw the error of his ways.

"Marshal, as long as me and Ellie can get outta this, I'll drop it. I'll let you have Haney, so long as he pays for what he done."

"I can't guarantee it, but I'll do my job, Cooley." Horne checked the side of the Nest, where a small, dark alleyway hid anyone who might intend to lurk and surprise him. Nothing.

Travis Cooley dropped his gun. Just then, someone appeared behind him in the Marshal's Office and whacked him right on the back of the head with a pistol butt. Cooley fell sack a ton of bricks and rolled down the front stairs of the Marshal's Office. He landed in the dirt of Main Street. Ellie screamed, but the hand that covered her mouth stifled most of the noise. Behind her, holding hot iron to her face, was Micah Haney. Horne raised his pistol to meet Haney's figure.

"Drop that girl, Haney, or I swear to God, you'll die this night!"

Haney laughed cruelly. "Marshal, you got no chance in killing me. Cooley's out cold and Ellie here'll keep you from thinking otherwise. You're old, anyways."

"I'm old, sure, but have I lost a step? You want to find out?"

Just then, two men appeared behind Horne. Haney looked surprised. Horne turned to see Ben Webb, who was held upright with help from Ezra Peck. Both men looked afraid, but with a tinge of anger at the man who had caused both of their lives trouble.

"Micah," Webb spoke in his baritone voice, "You got something comin' from me, boy."

Haney looked confused, "Mr. Webb… I…"

Peck interrupted Haney. "I told him about what you did, two years back, Haney. I saw you loosened his cinch and leave him for dead."

Haney's confusion faded and a sinister grin appeared. "And? What difference does it make? With Webb gone, I could make the Slanting W the best damned ranch in the state."

"It already is," Webb declared proudly. "But with you dead, it'll sure be nice having my neighbor back."

"What? You hate Peck," Haney pointed out.

"I only hate him because of the lies you fed me, fed him, for the past two years. And now, you holding that gun to my daughter's neck." Webb balanced himself on Peck's shoulder.

"Daddy…" Ellie sputtered but Haney clutched her neck and shut her up.

"Don't you dare hurt her, you sunofabitch!" Webb shouted as he tried to run toward his daughter.

"I'll do what I want, you old fool!" Haney spat. "I've the advantage here."

Webb started to tear up. "But why, Micah? I don't understand. I treated you like a son, even tried to get Ellie to take an interest in you. Why try to kill me? You'd get the ranch when I'm gone."

Haney was quiet. He hadn't expected sentiment from Ben Webb, just unadulterated hatred. The change in tone surprised him.

Meanwhile, Horne had made a slow, but steady movement toward Travis Cooley, who still lay unconscious on the ground. Horne checked on him, and saw that he was breathing.

"It don't matter now, Mr. Webb. I've gone too far to stop now."

"No, you haven't…"

"Yes, I have…" Haney confessed. "I kilt Jasper, and Peck's man, too."

"Why?" Asked Peck.

"I tried to recruit Jasper to my cause the day prior, and he spurned me. Said Webb was his boss, not me. Had to get rid of him, in case he spilt his guts. As for your hand, Peck, he was just in the wrong place at the wrong time. I had a meeting set up to sell them horses of ours, but that damned dumb cowhand started get fishy, asking questions and all. Decided to ride out back to the Tipping E, so I had to get rid of him, too."

Webb pleaded for his maddened foreman. "Well, Haney, you killed two men, did a lot of wrong, but you have a chance to save a girl's life by letting Ellie go."

"I know, but she's my ticket outta here."

"Then go! And don't stop riding till you're outta the Emerald Valley," Peck threatened.

Horne tried to make a slow movement toward the side of the Marshal's Office, but Haney caught sight of him and pointed his pistol at him.

"Don't try it, Marshal."

"Haney, you are outta options. Put her down, leave, and maybe I won't catch ya."

Haney thought it over for a second then shrugged. "Nope. Can't do it."

"What, why?" demanded Webb.

"I want the Slanting W, and I aim to have it."

"No!" Ellie cried out.

"All right, all right," Webb agreed. "Done!" The old man fiddled in his pockets for a moment.

Haney pointed his gun at Webb, thinking he might be concealing a weapon. Then, Webb pulled out a small piece of folded paper.

"I brought the deed. I thought this was what you might be after."

Webb took the pen from his pocket, unfolded the paper, and used Peck's shoulder to sign it.

"There, it's done." Webb waved the deed at Haney.

Haney looked to Horne. "All right, Marshal, I ain't gonna ask you to drop your gun, 'cause I know you won't, so I'm gonna trail this pistol on Ellie and I'm gonna get that deed. Then, I'm gone on the first horse I see."

"Just know, I'll comin' for you."

Haney smiled at the Marshal. Then he slowly started moving down the stairs and into the street with Ellie tight in his grasp. Webb outstretched his hand and Haney snatched the deed from it. Haney started backward down the street.

"Let her go, Micah!" Webb begged.

As Haney reached the horse tied to the hitching post outside the Nest, he threw Ellie to the ground. Then he jumped into the saddle and lit out down Main Street toward the livery stable and corral. Horne ran down the street after him, aimed his pistol, and took a shot. It winged the murderer in the right arm. He nearly fell off the horse, but kept himself up and going. While Webb and Peck attended to Ellie and Cooley, Horne watched Haney disappear around the corner.

At the end of town, Haney stopped his horse and dismounted. He ran to the corral, lifted the gate, and fired three shots into the air above the heads of the horses inside. Startled, the dozen scared horses came running down Main Street towards the Marshal and the others. Horne turned and shouted at them, trying to get their attention. In the confusion, Peck dragged Webb away from Ellie, leaving the girl in the middle of the street.

As Horne approached the Nest's porch, he saw her.

"Ellie!" Horne heard the frightened father cry out.

The horses were getting closer, their thundering hooves sounding like a storm. The mixing of mares and studs collapsed into one swarm of flesh and blood. Their nostrils flared, foaming at the mouth, afraid to die and afraid to run. But run they did, their natural instincts taking over.

Horne prepared to rush toward Ellie and grab her up, but from the other side of the street, Travis Cooley came in like a blur. Just as he did, the stampeding horses covered him and Ellie in a sea of hooves. Webb and Peck stared into the chaos, unable to help in any way. Horne lifted his head, peered around either side, but could not see Cooley or the girl. After a moment, the horses were gone, and left behind was a giant cloud of dust.

"Ellie!" Webb kept shouting as he tried to walk by himself. He was unsuccessful. Peck struggled to keep him upright.

Horne stared through the disintegrating dust cloud until a pair of figures appeared in the street. He frowned, thinking the young lovers had not made their way out of the stampede. Then: movement. Slowly, Cooley and Ellie rose from the ground and made their way through the remaining dust. Ellie ran to her father and embraced him.

Horne smiled at Cooley, who wiped his brow and realized his entire body was covered in dust.

"Didn't think you'd made it, boy."

"There for a second, thought we didn't, either. Luckily, we jumped to the side just in time." Cooley grinned through the dust covering his face.

With all well in town, Horne looked back toward the end of the street. Haney was nowhere in sight, but Horne knew he couldn't have gotten far. Horne had one thing in his favor; he knew this land, better than almost anyone in all of Emerald Valley. He wasn't the oldest, or the best scout, but he rode these hills day after day. Just then, someone stumbled out of the Marshal's Office. Horne saw Seth Barr standing in the doorway. Horne ran up the stairs and caught him before he collapsed.

"Seth, my God, are you all right?"

Seth coughed a bit. He looked like Haney had put the beating to him. There was a smear of blood on the sleeve of his right arm.

"How bad is it?"

"Just winged me, Marshal. Really ain't nothing but a big scratch."

Horne contemplated staying with Seth and going after Haney tomorrow. But his deputy wouldn't have it. "Marshal, go get 'im. I got this place covered."

Horne nodded and called over Cooley. He told the ranch hand to get the doctor for Seth. Then, Horne ran to one of the ponies hitched in front of the Marshal's Office. It was Seth's mare, a blue roan named Betty. She didn't care for being ridden, but if you could get on her she could fly. That's all Horne needed now. He tipped his hat to the onlookers and then bolted out of town.

✪✪✪

In the dark, rolling hills that cradled Talon's Crossing, Horne found himself nearly blind and using the moonlight through the trees to find his way. Horne followed the typical path out of town, northwest toward the high desert of western Nevada. A man could lose himself, and the world, in country like that. Hell, if he were fine with an Indian squaw for a woman, a man never really needed to leave such a place. That is, if he had something to hide from. Horne rounded a bend in the trees and pulled his rifle from its scabbard. He sensed he would find his target soon.

Another ten minutes, fifteen, maybe twenty or thirty, Horne couldn't be sure of the time now, he found himself riding up a rolling hill where the trees were swept clean from the prairie by the wind. Horne stopped the mare on the hillcrest, as she needed a breather and he wanted a look around. In the moonlight, the shadow of the horse and rider was clear against the blue background of night. Suddenly, a shot rang out. Horne fell from his horse, rolling down one of the sides of the hill.

When Horne found his bearings, his rifle was gone, but he was uninjured. He had fallen and rolled to avoid being shot at again. Hopefully, it would draw out the attacker—Haney—like a salve draws poison from a wound. Horne stayed perfectly still, crouched on the open hillside with his pistol in his hands. Another shot rang out. Horne fell to the ground. Another shot. Dirt kicked up right next to his head. Haney could see him!

Horne rose and ran backward toward the trees, turning to give himself the best chance of making it to cover. Another shot. It sounded like a rifle. Horne saw the row of trees ahead of him. He dove. Horne found himself crouched behind a tree, sucking in air as quietly as he could. It was tough, especially at his age. Another shot, but it flew through a pair of trees twenty yards to his right. Haney had lost him. Horne knew it was an equal playing field again. He checked his pistol in the moonlight for dirt. It was clean and ready.

Suddenly, a figure appeared in the distance, through a jagged row of crooked trees. In the moonlight, it looked like the light was being thrown onto the man that stood some twenty-odd yards away from him. Horne raised his pistol and pointed it at the center of the chest. His finger touched the trigger. He fired but the figure disappeared behind a tree and faded into darkness. Horne cursed under his breath and lowered his pistol. He didn't want to give away his position with another shot.

Horne crouched and walked, with feet as light as he could muster, around to the left. He hoped to cut off Haney in the next clearing of trees back toward town. Fifty yards passed by like nothing, and then Horne stopped. Ahead of him, Haney was standing next to a bent tree, the branches covering his body like a spidery hand. Horne raised his pistol and pointed, but could not get a clear shot. He contemplated taking his chance, but his surprise would be gone. He held his pistol outstretched, an extension of his own arm, thinking harder about taking a shot than anything he could remember. A man's life, Horne's own life, was on the line.

Then, fate intervened. From the clearing to their left, a man on horseback came toward them, a rifle blaring at Haney's figure. Haney fired back with his own rifle. In the scuffle, the rider was thrown from the horse and hit the ground with a thud. Horne thought it might be Cooley, or Peck, and ran toward the scene to help. When he arrived, what he saw surprised him. Lying on the ground was Ben Webb, covered in dirt and his own blood. Haney had managed to get him right in the gut, a good, or lucky, shot. Webb coughed up blood.

Haney was standing opposite Webb, and had not seen Horne. Haney was limping, as Webb had managed to get his own shot in, too. Horne noticed Haney's injured right arm, and that he had a hard time holding his rifle. It would be unlikely he could draw his pistol very well. As Haney approached Webb, the old man grabbed the rifle's barrel directed at him and tried to pull it away. Haney kicked Webb in the gut and then again in the side of the head. The old man coughed blood.

Haney raised his rifle and pointed it, as best he could, at Webb's body.

"Haney!" Horne stepped from the shadows into the moonlight. His pistol was pointed at Haney.

"Marshal." Haney's voice was tired. "I thought I got you back there."

"You didn't get anybody, Haney. Now, it's over. Drop your rifle!"

Haney considered the command for a second, but he had come too far. He owned the Slanting W, legally, and had nothing but open plain in front of him. All that stood in his way was an old lawman. He could take him.

Horne kind of hoped he would try it.

"Sorry, Marshal, but I've got to get going now. Drop that pistol and I'll leave you be. Get him some help." He pointed at Webb with the rifle.

"Sorry, but I can't do that. You, or both of us, will die here tonight."

Haney stared at Horne, and realized he was telling the truth. He sighed. "All right, then."

It happened so fast. Haney's rifle raised, half-turned because of his limp, right arm. Haney's shot. Webb's groan. Horne's shot. It was all over in a millisecond. In the end, Haney lay dead on the ground next to Webb, and Horne stood tall, his pistol barrel pouring smoke. When Horne was certain Haney was done, he holstered the gun and ran over to Webb.

"Damn you, old man," Horne futilely tried to push the blood back into the wounded man's belly.

"Old man? I took him out, didn't ya see?" Webb managed a weak smile. "Thank you, Marshal."

"For what?"

"For saving my girl, for making sure that animal never returns. And for saving my ranch." Webb coughed again, and groaned.

Horne smiled as much as he could, then had a thought. He crawled over to Haney's body and pulled the deed from the dead man's shirt pocket. Back with Webb, he opened it and held it up for him to see.

"This is yours, Ben. Again."

Webb smiled and then clutched the deed and Horne's hand at the same time. "Thank you. Please give it to my daughter, and son-in-law."

"I will," Horne promised as Ben Webb closed his eyes for the last time.

✪✪✪

As the red, morning sun crawled up the side of the Jarbidge Mountains and shone down on the Emerald Valley, the townsfolk of Talon's Crossing weren't waking up. They had been up all night, protecting their families from stray bullets, rounding up a corral of horses, and getting help for those who could still use it. When Horne returned to town with the sun, he had two bodies more than he had left with. One was stripped of all valuables and given a generic marker in the cemetery. No one spoke his name; no one said a blessing, other than Reverend Hanson, the only participant in the funeral.

Attended by his small family and larger supply of friends from the Valley, Ben Webb received quite the wake. Reverend Hanson presided, with Marshal Horne and Deputy Marshal Seth Barr watching over. His daughter Ellie, with Travis Cooley, Ezra Peck and his sons, and the rest of the Slanting W and Tipping E ranch crews were in attendance. Everyone shared their stories, their laughs, and their tears. In the end, he was a hero. He saved his family, and his ranch. In a place like Talon's Crossing, where men made their fortune in friends and acres, it was the greatest gift he could give.

Johns was busy for a few days, but then went back to shoveling horseshit at the livery. Ezra Peck was forced to seek out a new foreman, as Travis Cooley no longer needed the job. His new wife, Ellie, and ranch, the Slanting W, would take up most of his time. The Peck boys decided to take up the co-foreman position, much to their father's delight. After all, a man couldn't get to know his land from the inside of a living room. With the futures of both ranches secure, Peck and the new owners of the Slanting W, Ellie and Travis Cooley, reaffirmed the pact Peck and Ben Webb had made so many years ago. For many years after, the Cooleys and the Pecks continued to stock their herds with the wild horses descended from the Spanish inquisition.

"Well, Marshal, looks like things are starting to get back to normal," said Seth Barr, from his chair on the front porch of the Marshal's Office.

Marshal Gideon Horne sat at his desk, staring at the pink setting sun in the window.

"Yep." Horne was quiet today, a bit lazy and content with life and his job.

"Wonder when we're gonna have a bit more fun?" Seth spit into the spittoon.

"Hopefully, not again till Talon's Crossing is guarded by Marshal Barr," Horne grinned.

"Whew, that's a long time," Deputy Barr claimed wistfully. He stared out over the town, empty of activity but full of life.

It didn't take long for calamity to arise again in Talon's Crossing and the Emerald Valley. Marshal Horne, with his deputy and the dedicated townsfolk at his side, would confront it each and every time it crossed their path. For now, they had some downtime, and were content to enjoy it until they could no longer.

THE END

THE STAIN OF CORRUPTION

The slew of horses chomped at their bits, gushing their teeth against the cold metal. The saddle cinches chafed under the extreme speed at which they were traveling through the tight mountain pass. The warmth of their insides permeated through their skin and gave off a hot steam that wafte up and drifted through the cold air of wintertime.

For days the group of six horses and riders had been traveling south through the Jarbidge Mountains from the northern territories. What they were fleeing was known only to the riders, as the horses were content to work without a purpose. An occasional rest, with a few oats thrown in, was all the animals needed to keep their legs churning through the long days and short nights.

The riders, on the other hand, kept a wary eye on the trail behind them. What was chasing them wasn't visible to their eyes, but something told them they were not alone. After some time in the foothills of the Jarbidge, the riders became aware of the trail ahead that had opened up into a wide range of rolling hills.

"Pretty wide valley ahead of us," said one gruff man wearing a large wool overcoat, his hat slung low over his eyes to shield his face from the icy wind.

One of the other riders walked his steed up beside him, and replied, "Sure is, Davey. Bet this place is a pretty green in the Spring."

"Too bad we won't be here to see it, huh, Jim?" Davey snorted and shot a rocket toward the ground.

Davey didn't respond. He had been overtaken by the leader of the company, a man wearing a fine, black coat and a black bowler hat. The man's eyes were scanning the horizon beyond the foothills into the far valley below.

"Where we headed to, Vance?" Davey's voice cracked with slight terror.

"We're in the Emerald Valley," said Vance; his pony eager to continue on. "Not but one town for a few days ride."

"We stoppin' in for a spell?" Jim's voice reeked of terror, too.

"Got no choice," Vance told them. "These horses is beat. Been on the

67

run for three damn days, now. Need water, rest. That town's just a half day into the Valley."

"What about the law?" Davey asked. "What if they got a telegram or somethin' bout us?"

Vance was quiet for a second before replying. "Don't matter. We got by the law before. We will again."

Vance hollered out to his five riders and then kicked his horse into movement. The other riders followed quickly behind him as they descended down into the Emerald Valley. The cold followed the riders and their team as they wove a path through the countryside.

✪✪✪

Marshal Gideon Horne stood leaning against one of the wooden posts that kept his office upright. A stout man, thickly built and tall, Horne wore gray slacks, a white cotton shirt, and a fraying, green wool sweater under his black frock coat. A six-sided brass star on his lapel read: "Marshal — Talon's Crossing." A graying goatee surrounded his thick cheeks and his black Boss of the Plains was slung low over his eyes to keep the setting October sun from hitting his eyeballs. He was chewing on a piece of jerky that he brought for a snack after lunch. He watched a lone wagon make its way down Main Street heading out toward the east section of the Emerald Valley.

"Marshal!" Shouted someone from the other side of the street. It was Deputy Seth Barr, who was running as he yelled, the jockeying of his body causing his words to spill from his mouth like a barrel of loose nails.

Horne didn't move, but continued chewing on the jerky.

"Marshal!" Barr jumped up the steps of the office and caught himself before he ran into Horne. "Marshal…" Barr bent over, catching his breath with slow heaves of his chest.

"Spit it out, Deputy Barr." Horne smirked a little as he swallowed the last of his jerky. He placed his hand on his hip, just above the holster that held his nickel plated Colt revolver.

Barr coughed once before speaking. "Mayor Halliday is makin' plans to speed up the election to the first of November instead of Thanksgiving. If he does that, Bishop says Halliday'll surely take the election and Flanagan, well, he'll have no chance."

Horne had not moved since Barr's explanation began and stared at him the entire time. He wasn't a man to quickly judge anyone, let alone his only deputy. While Barr was green, he had good intentions and was an active employee. Horne would take an eager greenhorn over a lackadaisical hand any day.

The thought of Mayor Halliday moving up the election had corruption written all over it, a familiar stench since he took over office last Thanksgiving. The previous mayor of Talon's Crossing—Jim Reed, a proud yet determined representative—had taken sick and died just before the last election. The lack of any competition made it only too easy for Halliday to secure the election.

Although the "Mayor" of Talon's Crossings was more ceremonial than legislative, Halliday had slowly garnered himself more and more power. In December, a string of cattle thefts just outside of town forced the town elders to grant Halliday the power to regulate cattle sale locations. In March, the lack of fresh wheat crops gave Halliday the idea to stockpile the town's resources under the protection of the mayoral office. In July, at the annual Fourth of July celebration, Halliday forewent the fireworks in favor of an update to the mayoral coffers. All of this came at much chagrin to the townsfolk of Talon's Crossing, but they were simple and busy people who didn't have time to worry about such things.

Of course, Horne, and Deputy Barr to a lesser extent, suspected Halliday of corruption. A slew of miscreants had found their way into town since Halliday's ascension to power and the town itself became a much wilder place. Horne found himself busier with drunken disputes and public disturbances than ever before. He had not openly acted against Halliday yet, as Horne knew he needed to strike at the right moment to rid Talon's Crossing of Halliday and his corruption for good.

"Well, Marshal? Should we stop him?" Barr's breath had returned and his face, a lean and pale diamond shape, was twisted into a look of confusion, awaiting answer.

"No." Horne moved past Barr and walked down the steps of the office toward the street.

Barr followed after him. "But, Marshal, if we…"

"Deputy, Mayor Halliday's tactics are… unique, to say the least. But we don't need to stir up the coals because it only…" Horne's words trailed off as the thundering sound of horse's hooves approached the east end of town. "… starts a fire."

Five riders on horseback became visible on the east end of town, just past the corral. They approached at a swift pace, unrelenting until they passed Peabody's Livery and noticed the Plains Hotel on their right. One rider separated himself from the rest and walked his pony, a regal black stallion, toward the Eagle's Nest. The rider dismounted, tied up the reins, and walked toward the Nest.

Horne and Barr watched them all from the front of the Marshal's Office. While Barr was inspecting the four riders at the Plains Hotel, Horne's eyes were trained on the rider who had separated himself, obviously the leader. The man walked with a confident stride, and was tall and long-limbed. He wore all black except for a green undershirt and silver vest. On his hips were a matching pair of Ivory-handled Schofield revolvers turned backward.

Horne didn't recognize the face. A dark complexion—a hint of Indian possibly, or just too many days in the saddle—was mostly hidden by a low slung black bowler hat. He couldn't have been over thirty, but he walked with the confidence of a man who had seen quite a bit in those years. Horne decided to follow him into the Nest to check him out. Barr followed.

A few moments after the stranger disappeared through the doors of the Nest, Horne and Barr ascended the raised porch steps and entered. The atmosphere inside the Nest was an acquired taste. Mostly dark due to a lack of windows, except for a single one on the West-facing wall of the building, the main room was filled with oil lamps and a large stone-hearth fireplace on the East wall. Tables filled with gamblers and drunks lined the floor and a myriad of saloon girls traveled the tight places between them.

Horne's appearance in the doorway caught the attention of a few people sitting nearby and they gave a grunt to alert a few friends. Barr kept a close eye on Horne's blindside, following closely behind him as they weaved through the sea of tables and bodies. As Horne caught up with the stranger, who had been delayed getting to the bar by an active saleswoman, Mayor Halliday appeared standing on top of the bar.

Mayor Thomas C. Halliday was a forty-something man of slender build. He wore a tight-fitting gray suit, but his jacket was off and his sleeves rolled up. His hair was oily and slicked back and his face clean shaven. He stumbled trying to balance himself on the bar counter but a bystander caught his boots and helped him stay upright.

"Ladies… and gentlemen… may I have your attention, please!" Hollered Halliday. A moment later, assisted by a few "hushes", the place went silent. "I am Mayor Thomas Cromwell Halliday, formerly of Virginia City by way of Bakersfield. Although I come from a high-bred family in the golden fields of California, I was entranced some odd years ago by the green valleys of Nevada and, I am happy to say, now call the Emerald Valley my home."

Halliday had not grown up in the Emerald Valley, but businessmen in the region knew of his practices long before he arrived five years ago. Horne had heard about a tramp kid from California who swindled some horse traders in Virginia City about eight years prior, but was unsure if it was Halliday. No one in Talon's Crossing could truly account for his history or business engagements. His only real friends were a select few residents of town that became enamored by Halliday's presence and dramatics.

One such follower was Enos Long, a blacksmith's apprentice in town. An orphan kid, Enos was known around town as willing to do anything for a quick buck. Although he mostly used it to buy food and clothes, Enos had been long suspected of an opium addiction. Missing money and jewelry, and a generally odd disposition, made Enos the ire of many housewives and dutiful husbands of Talon's Crossing. Enos was a chubby boy of eighteen, but solidly built from the waist down. He was standing at the end of the bar, staring up at Halliday, smiling through crooked teeth.

"As the duly elected mayor of Talon's Crossing, it is my duty to inform you that, just this morning, I was informed by the respected elders of town that I have been granted temporary powers of declaration in Talon's Crossing!" Halliday ended his speech with quite a stir of fervor. The crowd around him, while unaware at what this meant exactly, cheered alongside him nonetheless. The louder you were, Horne came to know, the more people tended to agree. Ignorant people, at least.

"With this newly consecrated power of declaration, it is my first act as mayor of Talon's Crossing to declare a state of undue financial burden on the poor townsfolk." Halliday puffed out his lower lip on the last words. "As such, I will be enacting a ten percent tax on all liquor sales in saloons and restaurants inside town limits. This tax will be levied and stored for the future use of emergencies befalling the townspeople of Talon's Crossing!"

Again, Halliday's words echoed throughout the tall ceiling of the Nest and the crowd around him enveloped him with cheers. Halliday announced a round on the mayoral office and each man pushed his way to the bar to receive his free beer or shot.

Suddenly, the front doors to the Nest slammed open and a lone man entered. He was a huge man with thick arms and legs that spread from his trunk like the limbs of a great oak tree. He wore a dirty pair of leather breeches and a white-turned-brown shirt. He was covered in soot. His face was grim and covered in a thick black beard. He stood silent on the threshold of the door until someone noticed him and brought it to the Mayor's attention.

Halliday, still standing on the bar, turned and faced the man in the doorway. As he did, he jumped down from the bar and the mass of men separated for him like the Red Sea. He smirked, took a few steps forward, then stopped. Enos was at his right.

"Bloody Jim Flanagan," Halliday declared loudly. The name struck a chord of terror in the room and every man fell silent. A few saloon girls left their clients and walked toward the stairwell on the West wall of the building. "What brings you out of your lair?"

Flanagan was a blacksmith in town. Enos had been his apprentice for some time before Halliday arrived and acquired his services. Flanagan had a violent past, known then as "Bloody" Jim Flanagan. He did time in prison for his crimes, and started a new life in Talon's Crossing nearly ten years prior. Since becoming a member of the township, the people had taken to his steadfast and loyal ways, and tended to overlook his seedy past. It wasn't until Halliday arrived that they had been reminded of Flanagan's past.

"I hear tell you have swindled your way into another misuse of power in Talon's Crossing," Flanagan pointed a finger at the Mayor. His voice was guttural, and deep, but each word was eloquently pronounced.

Halliday laughed. "Misuse of power? Me? As mayor of Talon's Crossing? I possess only the power given to me by the elders of this great town. And rarely do I use them."

Flanagan didn't laugh. "Rarely do you use them?" He stepped forward and two nearby men backed up. "What of the Fourth of July party or the stockpile of crops in your barn? I'm sure your *mayoral* coffers are a bit plump, too, Halliday."

Flanagan kept walking until he was within arm's range of Halliday, who had no choice but to stand his ground in such a public venue.

Halliday began to speak, but Flanagan cut him off. "And now I hear you plan to surprise us townsfolk by moving up the mayoral election from Thanksgiving to the first of the month?"

"Yes, I do. That's true. Upon further inspection, we determined the election would receive better attention by concerned citizens when it's not placed so closely to a time of thanks and giving."

"Halliday, you know *damn* well that I am planning a mayoral campaign against you, and, if I was a betting man, which I am not, I would be inclined to bet that you plan to rig the election and cheat me out of the due election process."

"Are you callin' me a cheat?" Halliday queried through clenched teeth. He carefully leaned in toward Flanagan's head. They were roughly the same height. Halliday smiled. "Funny, comin' from a man who was once called the "Butcher of Boise". How many good men, women, and children did you *slaughter* Flanagan, before you decided to live a peaceful life as a lowly blacksmith?"

Flanagan clenched his fists and leaned in, pushing his forehead against Halliday's. "Clearly, one less than I should have."

Marshal Horne pushed a man aside and stepped beside the two raging bulls. Everyone who recognized him began whispering. Horne did not touch either man, but stared at them equally, shifting his eyes from one to the other. Flanagan caught Horne out of the corner of his eye and relaxed a bit.

"Gentlemen, for two mayoral candidates, I believe this debate has become a little heated." Horne kept both hands at his side, ready for action at any moment. Barr was behind him, to the left, eager to assist.

Finally, Halliday rescinded and agreed. "I believe you're right, Marshal Horne." He smiled. "Enos, let's return to our drinks." He turned away from Flanagan and walked back toward the bar, where a group of men were eager to share in another drink with the mayor.

Flanagan stared at Halliday until the Mayor disappeared behind the collection of bodies. He turned and left. Horne gave chase, but remembered his original target: the man in the bowler hat. Horne turned back to the crowd, scanning the faces and heads of the assembled, but was unsuccessful. Somewhere, among the myriad of saloon girls and drunkards, the newcomer had disappeared.

✪✪✪

Outside, the weather had taken a turn for the worse. A flurry of snowfall covered the cold packed dirt of Main Street and the temperature was dropping quickly. Horne looked up across the street, to his own office, where a small fire puffed whiffs of smoke out of the red chimney on top of the building. To the right of the jail was Flanagan's blacksmith shop. A small building stood behind the forge out front like a scared child behind a mean dog. Out front, Horne could see Flanagan pounding away at a hunk of iron despite the incoming weather.

Horne descended the stairs of the Nest and Barr followed. The duo made their way to Flanagan's shop and stopped a few feet from the front of the forge. The heat was deflecting the bitter bite of cold and made the covered porch over the forge emit a red glow and a subtle yet enduring warmth. Barr leaned his forearm against the wooden column that held up the porch.

"Flanagan." Marshal Horne's breath followed his voice like a cloud of blurred air, "Should I be worried about that stunt in the Nest?"

Flanagan kept pounding away at a hunk of iron. Sparks flew and hit Horne and Barr in the chest. The minute pieces of ore fell to the ground, hit the cold snow, and sizzled into nonexistence. Flanagan turned his back to the lawmen, dipped the iron into a bucket of water, and then returned it to the anvil. Horne couldn't make out what he was making, but wasn't distracted.

"Flanagan!" Horne raised his voice to make sure the large blacksmith heard him.

Flanagan stopped. He placed his hammer on the edge of the anvil and lifted the piece of metal he'd been working on to inspect it. He walked forward, away from the forge, and stopped when he was face to face with Horne.

"The stunt *I* pulled? Are you serious, Marshal? Do you see the sham Halliday is turning the mayoral office into?" Flanagan was serious, his white teeth flashing with each word like the brandishing of a sharp blade.

"Flanagan, I came to you because you're a reasonable man. A man with a past, like all of us, but a reasonable man, nonetheless. Halliday is not. We both know that." Horne finished with his hands on his hips.

"And what happens when he steals another mayoral election? What then, Marshal?"

"Wait a minute, are you insinuating that Halliday stole the election last year?" Barr interrupted.

"Just take a look at everything that cretin has done here in Talon's Crossing and I guarantee the stain of corruption is on it." Flanagan held up his metal work. It was an iron cross crudely melded together, the length of a man's forearm.

"What do you plan to do with that?" Barr asked.

"Plant it on his grave, Marshal," Flanagan answered; his eyes moving from Barr to Horne.

"And when do you intend to do that?" Horne's eyes narrowed.

Flanagan moved his right hand on an empty place on his hip, then clenched the same hand into a tight fist.

"No, Marshal. That life is behind me. But, you can bet that a man like Thomas Halliday doesn't last long in a wild land like this. There's always someone bigger, someone faster, and someone better."

Suddenly, a raucous sound echoed from the mountain pass to the east of town. All three men's eyes followed the sound to the area they heard it come from. A whiff of smoke billowed up over the edge of the buildings.

"What was that?" Barr was puzzled.

"No mining, for sure," Flanagan said.

"In weather this?" Horne pulled his chin whiskers. "Nothing good."

He began to walk toward his office but something stopped Horne. He was staring down toward the end of the street. The group of newcomers on horseback that had earlier setup outside the Plains Hotel were now gone. A slew of town folks flooded the front porches of the nearby buildings, all looking around to find the source of the loud boom. Mayor Halliday, followed by Enos, stumbled into the street.

"My God, what's happened?" Halliday called out.

"Something up in the Eastern pass," said a townsman who had walked over from the Plains Hotel.

"Sounded like a mine explosion," barkeep Jeff Hodges suggested.

"Hey," said the townsman again. "Isn't Hampton's mine up near there?"

"Yes," Halliday nodded. "It sure is."

"In this weather, you'd be hard pressed to find a mine in operation," Horne argued.

Flanagan agreed. "Too cold for digging."

"Not diggin' graves, eh Flanagan?" Poked Halliday. Enos smirked behind him.

Flanagan took a step toward Halliday. "Your grave, Mr. Mayor."

"That's enough!" Shouted Horne. "Any more lip from either of you, and I'll jail you on charges of public disruption and quarreling."

A lone horse and rider came galloping toward Main Street from the east end of town. He blew past a group of women outside Miss Fink's Restaurant and stopped his horse suddenly just past the Marshal's Office.

"Explosion! Explosion!" Cried the young man, who one townsman identified as Charlie Hampton, son of Tim Hampton, of mine fame. The boy was slender and wearing only a light jacket for such cold weather, obviously in a rush.

"Whoa, son, slow down," Horne held up his hands.

"What's happened up there, Hampton?" Asked another citizen.

"Explosion!" the young man shouted again, this time right in Marshal Horne's face.

"We know, son, but from what? Your daddy excavating in this weather?"

"No, sir, Marshal. Someone blew the mountain pass to smithereens."

A sudden wave of tension and fear arose in the collected crowd. Ideas of getting out, of staying in, and general chaos ensued. Marshal Horne allowed it for as long as he could, giving the folks of Talon's Crossing a chance to collect themselves before he began.

"Alright, alright listen up! If the Eastern pass is gone, that means the Western plains are the only way in and out right now, unless you're content in Talon's Crossing."

The land to the north and east of town was surrounded by the Jarbidge Mountains, and difficult if not impossible to traverse in such impending weather. To the south and west was the desert, where water was scarce, and a man took a chance without proper provisions. A small mountain pass to the east allowed horse and buggy to travel for most of the year, including winter. The cover of spruce pine allowed for some amount of protection from the elements.

"If the mountain pass is gone, we're all stuck here until further notice," Halliday stated the obvious. "Unless you want to brave the desert in such weather. As Mayor of Talon's Crossing, it is my duty to protect the fine citizens of…"

Flanagan snapped at him. "We can take care of ourselves, Halliday."

"Nonsense, Flanagan!" Said a townsman, "You might be warm and cozy in your forge, but what about wood for our fires and water for our cups?"

"Good point, Sid," said another man, a scar across his left cheek. "I had a shipment of wine headed this way, too. What am I gonna do?"

"Okay, okay, that's enough," Horne said forcefully. "We'll get it all squared away, but first things first. We need to figure out who exactly blew that pass."

"Maybe it was accidental?" Enos offered in a shrill voice.

"Accidental? Unlikely," Flanagan argued. "You don't just set off a charge that large by accident."

"So you're saying somebody *purposely* blew the pass?" Asked Sid. "Why would they do that?"

"Yeah, what would it do anybody any good keeping us stuck in town?" Repeated the scarred man.

Everyone was silent, except for a hushed whisper. Horne contemplated something, stewing on it before releasing it to the judgmental ears of the townsfolk. He stared at Halliday, then Flanagan, and finally looked back toward the Nest, where he had last seen the man in the Bowler Hat.

"There's only one reason somebody'd want to keep us in Talon's Crossing," Horne surmised aloud. Everyone turned to him and listened intently. "To make sure one of us never makes it out alive."

✪✪✪

"Nonsense, Flanagan!"

Marshal Gideon Horne found himself staring at a heap of logs piled against the inside walls of his office. They were the collected firewood they would have for their own fire until the mountain pass was cleared. Each member of the townsfolk had spent the rest of the daylight hours assembling their own firewood and all had ended with a less than stellar outlook on the next few days.

"Hey, Seth," Horne turned back to locate Barr in the back of the office.

Barr was rummaging through an old trunk full of blankets. He finally pulled one out, a wool blanket in the Indiana pattern of bright blues and purples.

He turned to Horne. "Yes, sir?"

"I've got a group of men getting some lanterns and provisions together to go up to the pass and see what they can do about those trees that fell and covered it." Horne glanced out the window to see a wagon being loaded with shovels and axes.

"I've not made a livin' off of double thinkin' your decisions, but do you think that's a good idea in the dead of night in this cold, Marshal?" Barr covered his upper half with the blanket and tucked it into his jacket.

"The sooner we get that pass cleared; the sooner folks can get home. The longer they linger here, the more wood and food we lose, and the quicker unrest sets in. But I agree, Seth, it's not smart sending them out in the dead of night. Especially with a potential killer hanging around." Horne walked over to the door, where a scarf was hanging on the hook. He grabbed it and threw it to Barr. "That's why I'm sending you with them."

Horne watched Barr descend the steps outside through the window, saddle up his own pony, and follow the wagon out of town eastward toward the mountain pass. When the wagon and its single lantern, bobbing back and forth in the moonlight, disappeared from view, Horne shed the blanket around himself. He lifted the handle on the front door and left for the Plains Hotel.

The Plains Hotel was the largest building in Talon's Crossing, and one of the oldest. It was founded in the years just after Henry Talon's founding of the Eagle's Nest, its next-door neighbor. Unlike the Nest, which came under new ownership every ten years or so, the Plains Hotel remained in the hands of one of Emerald Valley's oldest families: the Van Gelderens. Originally Dutch settlers to Pennsylvania, Joop Van Gelderen moved his family of eleven children with Henry Talon's party and settled down in the Emerald Valley alongside him. After Talon's disappearance in 1855, the Van Gelderens took over running the new township and remained an integral part of its lasting legacy.

Currently, Gerwin Van Gelderen was proprietor of the Plains Hotel. He looked up from a log book when Marshal Horne entered the front door and smiled. Gerwin was in his fifties, and frail for such a stout name. His pale skin seemed to hang off his cheekbones and the skinny mustache that lined his upper lip only accentuated his skeletal bone structure. He wore a black suit and tie, more reminiscent of a mortician than a businessman.

"Marshal Gideon Horne," Gerwin greeted, smiling. He had straight teeth stained yellow by years of poor care.

"Gerwin, good to see you," Horne nodded.

"What's all this commotion outside? The girls are upstairs gossiping about what's going on. What trick can I play on them today?"

"No trick, Gerwin, no trick. Someone blew the mountain pass east of town and we're all stuck here for the foreseeable future." Horne reached the front counter and leaned an elbow against it.

"Oh, I see. This is good for business, I think. Now we'll have sold out rooms." Gerwin pulled out the remaining room keys from a drawer beneath the countertop.

"I wouldn't rush to do so just yet," Horne advised. "We're low on resources, especially firewood. Unless you've got some oil or coal behind that door, you're gonna run out as soon as those tenants strike their matches for a nighttime fire."

Gerwin's smile disintegrated into a frown and he set the keys back in the drawer. "I see. This is not good, then."

"Yeah, that's why I'm here, Gerwin."

"Anything for you, Gideon." The Van Gelderens were a law-abiding folk, and likewise Horne had earned a good reputation among them. Gerwin and Horne had spent many a night talking around a pot of coffee.

"Well, I'm lookin' into a group of men that came into town earlier. Maybe four or five of them. Look like saddle tramps, mostly."

The mention of the men struck a chord. Gerwin's gulped, and he feigned a movement to leave, but stopped himself. Horne recognized it as fear, and something to be assessed in a man of Gerwin's usual calm demeanor. The Marshal knew Gerwin recognized the men, but what exactly Gerwin knew eluded him. Something within Horne kept him from asking any more questions about it. He suspected his life, and that of his friend, hung in the balance. He tipped his hat to Gerwin and left.

Outside, the wintry air had calmed, but the snowfall increased to a heavy fall. Horne suspected by morning Main Street would be at least an inch under snow. It complicated the situation, ensuring Barr and the others would be unsuccessful in clearing the pass by morning. It'd be another full day before the way could be cleared, most likely. Horne saw it as a mixture of gift and curse, them being stuck in town. They were trapped in Talon's Crossing with a potential killer, but, whoever he was, he too was locked in here with Marshal Gideon Horne.

As Horne veered toward his office, he caught sight of Jim Flanagan crossing Main Street carrying his iron cross. Flanagan was wearing his blacksmith's apron and his eyes retained the fire of his forge. Horne hurried up behind him and grabbed onto the iron cross. Flanagan didn't let go, and was able to pry the cross away from Horne.

"Don't do this, Flanagan!"

Flanagan turned back to Horne and, through gritted teeth, said, "That corrupt excuse of a politician has insulted me, and this town, for the last time."

"I can't let you do this, Flanagan." Horne tried to grab the cross again.

Flanagan suddenly let loose an elbow that connected with Horne right in the mouth. The lawman was sent stumbling backward, blood trickling from the places between his teeth. He spit out the blood onto the snow.

"I'm not asking, Marshal." Flanagan turned away and walked into the Nest.

As Horne collected himself and popped his jaw a couple times, a commotion began inside the saloon. Hollers rang out and a scuffle was heard through the plank walls. Horne pulled the nickel-plated Colt from his holster, spit out the last bit of blood he could, and ran inside.

A body came flying at Horne. He was just able to dodge it in time to stay on his feet. A flurry of punches and pushes began in the center of the room. Men backed up to the walls and began hollering and shouting. Horne moved past them and into the center of the "ring." Two men were holding Flanagan back by his arms while Enos repeatedly punched him in the gut. Mayor Halliday was holding the iron cross that Flanagan had made, twirling it between both hands and smiling as his minions did his bidding.

Horne pushed past Halliday, raised his pistol, and slammed the butt of the gun into the back of Enos' head. The boy fell to the floor unconscious. As Horne turned, he half expected the mayor to strike at him with the cross. But, the mayor stood still, smiling and twirling the cross between his hands. Horne re-holstered his pistol and prepared to clear the place. Jim Flanagan had other plans. With a vengeance, he pushed aside the two men holding him back and tackled Mayor Halliday to the floor.

Before Horne could separate the two, Enos was grabbing onto his legs. Horne tried to fight off the half-conscious boy, but his grip was sure. Horne caught a glimpse of Halliday and Flanagan rolling on the floor, throwing punches back and forth. A moment later, Flanagan had turned Halliday onto his face and locked a tight choke around his throat from behind. Then, without notice, a shot rang out in the saloon. Every man ducked his head and touched his iron, ready to strike back.

A man holding his gun pointed upwards walked through the crowd from around the bar. As the knock of his boots against the wooden floor signaled his approach, Enos let loose Horne's legs. Flanagan eased his grip on Halliday's neck. Enos rubbed the back of his head and the mayor rolled over on his belly, gasping for breath. A group of men parted and the shooter was revealed. He wore a black coat and bowler hat, and let his ivory-handled pistol fall nonchalantly back into its hip holster across from its twin.

"Bloody... Jim... Flanagan..." greeted the stranger. He tipped the front of his bowler and revealed a handsome face beneath it. His carved jaw was clean shaven and his blue eyes pierced through the darkness of the Nest.

Jim Flanagan pushed Halliday aside and rose up. He dusted himself off and walked toward the stranger.

"Bloody... Jim Flanagan..." said the stranger a second time. He smiled widely, splitting his face in two.

Flanagan's face turned from a reddish hue of anger to a flushed scarlet of surprise and fear. Slowly, his lips revealed two words, "Vance... Tillerson?"

Horne recognized the name from a wanted poster that hung in his office. The flier described Tillerson as a "gunman," wanted for "murder, debauchery, and thievery." Horne had heard the name before among his fellow lawmen, and never in a good light. Horne had dealt with men like Tillerson, and found only two ways to do so: run them out of town or, if need be, make sure they never leave.

"I thought when we left you bleedin' on that hot sand, you were dead and gone," Tillerson stared into Flanagan's eyes.

"A true brother wouldn't leave a man for dead," Flanagan retorted angrily.

"For dead? Jim, you had six bullet holes in 'yah, who was I to say you'd make it out of that alive?"

"Well, I did. And spent six years in the pen for my troubles."

The two bulls stared hard at one another, neither moving an inch. Horne stepped in and they slowly separated themselves. Flanagan turned away from his old comrade and exited through the doors of the Nest. Halliday was being helped up by Enos, whose bloody hair dripped on the floor.

"Now, let's all get some sleep," Horne ordered, turning to look at the multitude of men staring from the edges of the circle.

Halliday pushed past Enos and stared at Horne as he did, muttering. "Some of us gonna be sleepin' quite a long while after tonight."

Horne didn't respond. It was no use, not with the tension in the town and the potential for more violence. He watched Halliday and Enos make their way back to the bar. As Tillerson bent over to pick up the iron cross, Horne walked to him and extended a hand. Tillerson placed the cross in the lawman's open palm.

"Not gonna have trouble are we?"

Tillerson smiled coldly. "No, sir. I've never started trouble wherever I went."

Somehow, Horne couldn't believe that, but he'd save his breath for now. He needed to get back to the office and check on the warrants for Tillerson. He had to be sure before he made any moves. Horne gripped the iron cross and turned back to the doors.

Outside, the snow had set in hard. The air above town was thick and dark, and made it seem like they were in an oven, or a forge. In a way, it made sense to Horne, with everything that had gone on. His boots crunched two inches of powdery snow as he walked across the street to the office. He stepped inside and shook off the cold.

The fire was nearly out, and Horne stoked it with his poker. Once more he wrapped the heavy horsehair blanket around himself. He wasn't an old man, by any means, but he was naturally cold blooded and the warmth of the thick blanket gave him confidence. He sat down at his desk and opened a drawer. It was full of wrinkled papers bound together by a rubber band. He pulled them out and the faces on the page stared back at him. Each month, he received wanted posters, telegrams, and letters about wanted men and outlaws in or around his territory from the provincial marshal, territorial sheriffs, and Texas Rangers hundreds of miles to the south.

He sifted through some papers until he found "Vance Tillerson" written underneath the word "WANTED." He read the description: "Vance Tillerson, suspected leader of the Tillerson Gang, is wanted for murder, debauchery, and thievery in the state of Nevada, and the Utah and Arizona Territories. Tillerson is armed and dangerous, and never travels alone."

As Horne read the last word, a deep thud hit his front door. He glanced up, wondering who it could be. He'd had about enough of Flanagan and

Halliday's debacle, especially for two mayoral candidates. He knew it couldn't be Tillerson. He'd not be caught dead in a jail. Horne rose up from the chair and opened the door. The body of Seth Barr, his lone deputy, fell over the threshold.

Horne quickly dragged Barr into the office and then covered him with another blanket. His deputy was near frozen from the elements and as the blanket warmed his blood, he began to shake. Horne rubbed Barr's body with his hands and dragged him closer to the fireplace. After a moment, Barr's body began to take in the warmth and the shaking subsided a bit. This allowed Horne to lift the blanket and inspect Barr's body. One red stain was located on the left side of his abdomen. Horne turned his deputy over and saw the other end of the bullet wound and sighed. He would live with a clean wound like that, but it still needed to be cleaned and dressed immediately.

An hour later, after his wound had been attended to, Seth Barr sat sipping a warm cup of coffee on the bed inside the jail cell. He was coughing a bit, but the shaking was done. Horne leaned against the cell and waited for Barr to explain what happened to him.

"Well, Marshal," Barr finally started, "we was clearing trees and such when the snow really started to set in. Sid and Crowe wanted to turn back and skedaddle…" He coughed. "But I kept 'em workin', pitchin' in where I could, but keeping a close eye on the tree-line as we did, like you asked. Then, it started."

There was silence. Horne didn't prompt Barr to continue, as he knew it was a difficult thing. Horne had already concluded that Barr was the only survivor of the work crew. Still, he needed the details. It could mean life and death.

"Gunshots in the dark, horses running all around, men screaming and falling dead in the snow. Seemed like there were a hundred of 'em shootin' at us. I got hit fairly early and lost my pistol in the snow. I drug myself to the tree-line and hid out till the chaos ended. That's when I saw 'em hit the trail and leave."

"Did you get a good look at them?"

"Yes, sir. About four, or five, of 'em. No more. Ridin' hard and fast down the trail. All of 'em wrapped in big coats and blankets. I caught sight of one in the moonlight. A bright blue sheet, it looked like he was wearing to keep warm. I only caught it because it got loose and was fluttering behind him like a war banner."

"Where were they headed? What direction?"

"Here, Marshal. They was headed toward town."

The thought of these brutal killers already back in town after trying to kill his deputy made Horne's gut sink. He walked out of the cell and into the office. After pulling a Winchester 76 off the wall, Horne loaded it with a box of shells on his desk. Barr limped into the office, his shirt off and dressings visible on his abdomen.

"Marshal, I know it means these killers are here in town with us, but what are we gonna do against five skilled gunmen?"

"I don't know, Seth," Horne replied honestly. "But I've got to get over to the Plains."

"The Plains Hotel?"

"Yeah, I think Gerwin and his girls are in terrible danger."

"Really?"

"That blue blanket you saw flappin' in the wind? That's the same blanket they use at the Plains."

Horne finished loading the rifle, cocked it to check it was loaded, and then lowered the hammer back down for safety. He grabbed his black hat off the rack and put it on.

"I'm confused, Marshal."

"It they had hold of one of the blankets from the Plains Hotel, it means they're staying there, possibly holdin' the Van Gederlen's against their will. I was over there earlier, and got a funny feelin' like something wasn't right. And, if you saw them headed back to town, they might be there now."

Barr reached up for the other rifle off the wall, but grimaced in pain as he tried to lift his arm. Horne grabbed Barr and led him to the chair behind his own desk. He set him down gently. The marshal grabbed the rifle and then handed it to Barr.

"You stay here. There's more shells in the bottom drawer of the desk. Load it up and be ready for a fight. Even if I'm able to stop them from takin' more lives tonight, I'm sure one or two of 'em scoot out and run down Main Street. Pop open that window there and take 'em out if you can. No sense letting 'em run free and do more damage."

Barr's face crinkled into a reassuring smile, or what he could muster of one. Horne nodded and left. The brisk air of midnight hit the lawman in his face, and wished he hadn't shaved yesterday morning. He shivered and then gripped the rifle tighter to give himself some strength.

He could see the lights on inside the Nest and figured Mayor Halliday and his crew were still up and at 'em, bad-mouthing Flanagan, and now Horne for what he'd done to Enos. He hoped Halliday wouldn't be another problem he'd have to deal with. Either way, he knew he couldn't worry about it now. Gerwin and his family needed his full attention.

When Horne entered the Plains Hotel, it was quiet inside. Gerwin wasn't standing at the desk and most of the main lights were not lit. It was after midnight, but it was too quiet for a usually busy hotel. Horne kept his rifle at the ready as he passed the front desk and followed the hallway to the back of the building, where Gerwin and his family lived. He reached two doors, one to the washroom, the other to the family's bedroom.

Horne chose the bedroom, turning the handle on the door. He pushed it open slowly. The door creaked open and the lawman pointed his rifle into the darkness. Nothing. The room was empty. No sign of Gerwin, his wife, or his two daughters. Horne returned to the washroom door, but a sound above his head caught his attention. It was the shuffle of feet that did not want to be detected. Horne scurried to the stairwell back in the front foyer and began walking up the stairs.

At the first turn in the stairs, Horne lifted his rifle and led with the barrel. Nothing. He ascended the last flight of stairs and reached the top floor. A long hallway of rooms lay ahead of him. Every door was closed. Horne cursed under his breath, knowing the odds just became even higher against him walking out alive, let alone with Gerwin and his family safe in hand. He wished Barr was here to help.

As Horne took a step forward, a door burst open at the end of the hall, on the right side. A pistol appeared, blasting a bullet in his direction. Horne dove to his right, colliding with a door. The momentum and weight busted the door off the hinges and sent Horne falling into the room. He rolled off the door and looked around. It was empty inside. He got to one knee and readied to fire back. He pointed his rifle out, but no one was present.

He walked slowly out of the open doorway and aimed to the spot where the pistol had materialized. Suddenly, a door to the left burst open and another gun appeared. Horne dropped to his belly and fired at the wall to the left of the gun. The bullet went clean through the thin wall, struck the man holding the gun, and he stumbled out into the hallway. Horne cocked the lever action and blasted another shot. This one struck the man in the chest and he fell dead in the hallway.

This prompted another door to open and Horne rolled to the other side of the hallway, firing two shots in the direction of the second door. The barrage of lead bought Horne some time to jump up and into the room the dead man had come from. Inside, he cocked his rifle and waited for the gangs' next move. He hesitated, then decided to act. He saw another doorway across the hall labeled "Room #4." He knew Room #4 connected with Room #6 and made one large room. It was the only of its kind in the Plains Hotel.

Horne rushed across the hallway, past a barrage of bullets and dove into the door shoulder-first. The momentum shattered the hinges and he flew into the room. He landed on his side and had no time to collect himself, as a man was standing on the other side of the suite. Horne fired one, two, and finally three shots at the dark figure. One or two of the shots found their target and the man slumped back against the wall, dead.

The Marshal rolled off the door and got up. He heard the shuffle of feet along the other side of the wall, in the hallway. He cocked and fired a shot where he thought the man was standing. He missed, and the shuffle turned to a full run. The figure passed the open doorway and disappeared down the stairs. Horne cursed beneath his breath again, but hoped Barr would see him coming.

Horne counted in his head as he waited. Two dead, one gone. He knew there were five riders, from Barr's account. So, two were up here still. At least one was likely to be with Gerwin and his family, a gun to their heads. Horne knew the next few moves were important and he had to be careful. He got to his feet quietly and walked past the slumped man to the door of Room #6. He hoped the others wouldn't expect him to come through this door.

Before Horne could make his move, the door in front of him flew open and whacked him in the chest. The lawman was thrown backwards, dropping his rifle in the confusion. He hit the floor and slid backward. A gunshot rang out, and Horne rolled and kept rolling across the floor until he was behind the bed. He yanked his Colt free of its holster at the same time flipping the bed over. Then he dove to the left onto his side. He aimed his gun and returned a volley of bullets. The man across the room was struck in the leg and fell to his knees.

Horne rose to finish him, but the final man appeared in the doorway of Room #4 behind Horne's left shoulder. The man fired two shots, one narrowly missing the Marshal's head, and Horne returned two shots of his own. The gunman dove behind the bed against the other side of the wall. Between two active gunmen, Horne wasn't sure what to do. All that drove him in the moment was the blood pumping hard and fast through his veins, and the thought of Gerwin and his girls, tied up or worse in some room at the end of the hallway.

In the dark, he could hear the injured gunman limping away from the center of the room, dragging his injured leg with him. Horne judged the man was now standing in front of the window opposite the hallway. Horne looked at the bed next to his face; underneath the thin mattress was a frame of springs. Horne re-holstered his pistol and decided on his course of action. He grabbed the spring frame, lifted it off the wooden bed frame, and pushed it forward toward the injured man. The heavy bed, frame and all, collided against the man and he was thrown back against the window. The momentum pushed him through the thin glass and he disappeared into the darkness below.

Horne fell to the floor as the last gunman let loose more bullets, but they were late, missing Horne. Horne pulled his own pistol from his position on the floor and fired one shot right into the chest of the man across the room. The man clutched his chest, dropped his gun, and fell back dead.

Marshal Horne lay breathing in the deathly quiet of the Plains Hotel. Two dead men lay behind him, one across from him, and one in the hallway to his right. His heartbeat slowed to a regular pace, he holstered his gun, and stood up. He walked out of the busted doorway and followed the hallway to the last door at the end. As it opened, the faint light from the oil lamp inside revealed Gerwin and his family, tied to chairs side by side.

A few minutes later, Gerwin was freed and helping Horne cut the last bits of rope holding the women. Once freed, they embraced each other. Gerwin shook Horne's hand repeatedly, thanking him again and again. Horne nodded and tried to smile, but he had more business to attend to. There was another gunman still free in town, as well as the leader of the gang. Horne had a suspicion they had already met.

After making sure Gerwin and his family were safe, Horne descended the stairs and hurried to the hotel's front door. He intended to get to Deputy Barr and get ready for more battle. He was certain the rest of town would already have heard the commotion and gunshots. As he grasped the door handle, a pistol cocked behind him and the barrel pressed against the back of his neck.

✪✪✪

"Let go uh that thar' door handle, you cocky lawman," the gruff voice commanded. A hand reached across Horne's body and pulled the pistol from its holster. "Now, turn 'round and walk toward the parlor."

Horne fired one shot right into the man's chest.

Horne turned and looked down into the eyes of Enos Long, who was holding his own gun against Horne's chest. The lawman contemplated trying to disarm him, but he wasn't sure how skilled Enos was, or how mad.

"I can guess why you're doin' this, Enos. But does your master know what you're up to?"

Enos laughed as he shoved Horne into the parlor. Sitting at the first table was Mayor Thomas C. Halliday. He had a few scratches on his face and was looking a bit more defeated and volatile than usual. He was spinning the cylinder of his Colt Peacemaker.

"Ah," said Horne, "So your master knows."

"I do," Halliday chuckled. "I set 'em on the task."

"You're a changed man when you're not in the public eye," Horne pointed out.

"As every elected official is," Halliday stood up from his chair. He was still fiddling with his pistol. "Even you, Marshal."

"Don't compare us, Halliday," Horne snapped.

"Either way, a politician's got to know his constituents," Halliday continued. "And I know you're not going to be throwing my name in the ballot box."

"How's that? I've got a few more weeks to decide. I will say, though, this gun to my back thing ain't helpin' any."

"Well, Marshal," you shouldn't uh struck me last night." Enos cut in.

"Sorry 'bout that Enos, but you were beatin' on a helpless man," Horne reminded him.

"Helpless man?" Enos coughed in surprise.

"Jim Flanagan, is hardly helpless, Marshal," the Mayor disagreed. "You do realize he's a ruthless killer who spent years in federal prison for murder?"

"I understand that, Halliday, but I also understand a man who has paid for his crimes, and created a new life in a town under my jurisdiction."

"He chose the wrong town."

A moment of silence broke their conversation. Each man was mulling over his next move.

"So," Horne said calmly. "What's next?"

"Next, you are going back to your office."

"Lettin' me go?"

"Hardly," laughed Halliday. "You'll be in a cell this time."

"A cell? What do you plan to do, run for marshal, too?"

"Not me. Him."

Halliday pointed to someone standing to the right of Horne, in the corner of the parlor. It was Vance Tillerson grinning, his bowler hat cocked to the side. He was leaning against the wall, and stepped forward when he was mentioned.

"Tillerson, huh?" Horne smirked. "So... a crooked swindler for mayor, and a wanted murderer for marshal? Talon's Crossing deserves better."

"You're right," Tillerson stepped toward Horne. "And that's why we're here. I knew you had recognized me, and would have it out for me here soon."

"Is that why you tried to have your boys take out my deputy and then coerced me into the Plains Hotel for an ambush?"

"Smart man," Tillerson nodded. "I see why you've made a name for yourself here. But that time's over."

"So are all your men."

"I can get more men, lawman. Then again, I really don't need men, not with the mayor here backing me for marshal after you're gone."

"You'll need all the help you can get. My deputy is posted up with a loaded rifle, and he's a crack shot with it, too. Former marksman in the Army Scouts."

The front door opened and Seth Barr stumbled in and fell to the floor. Behind him stood a gruff man in a wool overcoat. Horne assumed it was the last of Tillerson's men who had escaped from the hotel.

"Good work, Davey," said Tillerson. Davey smiled.

"Sorry, Marshal," Barr said, looking up from the floor.

Horne tried a smile, "It's okay, Seth."

"You're out of men and out of time," Mayor Halliday said smugly.

With that, Enos pushed Horne toward the door. The marshal passed Barr and Davey, opened the door and walked into the street. Numerous people lined the main street talking and, likely, pondering where the gunshots had come from earlier. Enos shoved Horne forward with his gun jabbing into the Marshal's back. Thus it was hidden behind Horne's large frock coat.

Halliday stepped forward and addressed the townspeople standing there. "Gentlemen, the gunshots were our own Marshal Horne dispatching a group of cretins. He is wounded, but we are escorting him to his office to take good care of him."

One of the townsmen spoke up, "Nice work, Marshal!" A few other men joined in a quick cheer. They soon reached the marshal's office and ascended the steps. Next door a large figure emerged from the forge. The big man moved at a brisk pace toward them. Enos peered out from underneath the office porch, where a lantern exuded faint light.

"Who's there?" he called out.

Behind them, Barr and Davey were following, the outlaw holding up the Deputy. Tillerson and Halliday stood in the middle of the street.

Suddenly, a shot rang out. The shot struck Enos in the hip. From the sound, it was a .44, and the slug sent him flying backward to collide with the building wall. Horne used the opening, and launched his body backward. He hit Davey under the chin with the back of his skull. Davey fell clear off the porch into the darkness. Barr stumbled past Horne and dove into the doorway of the jail.

Another shot rang out, this time toward Tillerson and Halliday. Both men ran toward the end of the street near the livery. The gathering of townsfolk quickly dispersed, all looking to hide from the flying lead. Another shot, toward Tillerson, another shot, toward Halliday. Then, the shooter emerged in the lantern light next to the marshal's office. It was Jim Flanagan, carrying two pre-war Dragoons. He stepped up onto the porch and stood over Horne, who was lying on the wooden planks. He gave the Marshal a hand up.

"Let's take back our town," Flanagan suggested.

Barr stepped out of the office, carrying a pistol and a shotgun. He handed the pistol to Marshal Horne.

"Seth, let's get you back in that window, picking them off wherever you can," Horne directed. "Jim, you go out the backside of the office and make your way down to the livery. I'll hit the alley between the Nest and the Plains."

The three men quickly got to their duties. Horne looked down the street each way before he ran across and disappeared into the alleyway between the two prominent buildings. No one was left outside, and Horne hoped Tillerson and Halliday were not hiding in some other place. It would make finding them much more difficult. Horne reached the end of the Nest and looked to the left. A stray dog was picking garbage out of a box at the far end of the street.

Horne turned to his right, toward the livery, where he'd meet up with Flanagan. When Horne reached the end of the Plains Hotel, he looked down the alleyway and saw the limp body of the man he'd earlier pushed out the upstairs window. He continued on to Peabody's Livery. An old, broken carriage was sitting alone behind the building. The corral was a bit further ahead, but Horne didn't want to be caught in the open. He turned down the small alley between the livery and the corral, using the shadows of the building as cover.

As Horne neared the edge of the livery building, a flurry of shots rang out. Horne ducked his head back as one shot ripped through the wood next to his head. Across the way, he saw Flanagan fire back a volley toward the front of Ms. Fink's Restaurant. Horne ran out, barely escaping a slew of lead and dove behind a water trough in front of the livery.

"Flanagan!" Shouted Horne.

Flanagan hollered back, "Yeah!"

"You got an eye on 'em?"

"Yeah!" Flanagan took a moment to fire two more shots. "Someone's up by Ms. Fink's."

Horne peeked through a cracked board in the trough, and could see a figure moving in the faint light from inside Ms. Fink's. He couldn't tell who it was, but suddenly, the shots stopped. A voice rang out.

"Flanagan." It was Vance Tillerson. "Let's end this here and now."

"Fine with me," Flanagan shouted back.

Horne contemplated stopping him, or at least trying, but he knew it was no use. Men like Flanagan and Tillerson were too big to fit in the same world together. He was unsure of their history together, but he knew it had not ended well. In the life of outlaws, there was no honor amongst thieves. Jim Flanagan, at least, had paid for his wrongs and tried to change.

Tillerson emerged from behind Ms. Fink's porch, holding a pistol in his left hand. Horne could tell it was a Schofield. Flanagan walked out from behind the buildings across the street. He was carrying both his Dragoons. When Flanagan and Tillerson saw each other, they holstered their weapons and met in the center of the dirt avenue.

"You stand no chance, Jim Flanagan," Tillerson boasted.

"You've always been fast, Vance, but you're also overconfident."

"We'll see soon enough."

A moment of silence passed.

"Why'd you really leave me for dead?" Asked Flanagan.

"You know how it is, Jim."

"You wanted my share, huh?"

"As it is amongst outlaws."

"I paid for my crimes," Flanagan declared with justification.

"I heard."

"And now, you'll pay for yours!"

As both men prepared to draw, shots rang out. Mayor Halliday was running and gunning his way from the Plains Hotel to the Marshal's Office, fanning his pistol. Shots boomed from the window, where Seth Barr fired his double-barreled shotgun. They stopped Halliday in his tracks and he turned left toward Ms. Finks. Then, Davey jumped out from behind the wagon beside the Nest and started firing at Barr in the window.

In the commotion, Tillerson and Flanagan's duel was sidetracked and both men started running for cover. Flanagan jumped behind the porch at the Red River Restaurant, beside Ms. Fink's. Tillerson returned to his spot beside Ms. Fink's, where Halliday joined him.

Gideon Horne saw his opening. He ran down the front of Peabody's Livery under the cover of shadows and dove across the alleyway between the livery and the Plains. Davey turned and tried to fan a shot at Horne, but his cylinder clicked empty. Horne returned fire, winging Davey in the arm. Deputy Barr appeared in the office door, and released both barrels at Davey. The man was lucky and both slugs missed their mark.

Halliday and Tillerson fired their guns in sync, one time at Flanagan, then at Horne. Horne jumped onto the porch of the Plains and aimed his gun at Davey, who was running away from him across the street. Horne contemplated shooting him in the back, but his conscience kept him from pulling the trigger.

Davey made it across the street to the other side of Ms. Fink's porch. Horne moved off the porch and took cover behind the wagon that Davey had used earlier. He motioned Seth Barr to get behind the office porch, and his deputy complied. Horne reached for bullets on his gun belt, and found three. As he loaded them in, he realized knew the finish was coming. Someone was going to win, someone was going to lose.

Suddenly, Tillerson and Halliday were spooked, and ran out from the porch and into the street. A barrage of bullets followed them as Jim Flanagan appeared in the faint light, firing both Dragoons. Horne jumped out from behind the wagon and let loose two of his rounds. One struck Halliday in the leg and he fell to the ground. The other missed Tillerson.

Davey ran out and aimed at Horne, but Barr unloaded a shotgun round right in his back that sent him flying face-first into the snow. He jerked once, then was still.

Horne tried to follow Tillerson but the crooked Mayor disappeared between the Plains and livery. Halliday dragged himself toward his gun. Horne kicked it away from him and walloped him with the butt of his Colt.

Flanagan joined Horne, already reloading his cap and ball pistols. He cursed as he continued loading. Seth Barr was hobbling toward them.

"Sorry, Marshal," said Flanagan, "Thought I had 'em both."

"Well, two down, one to go," Horne tallied. He looked around, assessing the situation. "Alright, Tillerson's somewhere back there. Hardly any of the buildings have back doors. Jim, you go down the alley between the Nest and Plains. I'll take the livery and Plains. Seth, stay here in case he runs out."

Flanagan and Barr nodded in agreement. Horne took the alleyway and followed it toward the end of the building. As he rounded the corner, he remembered he had a single bullet left. He cursed under his breath at his stupidity, especially for an experienced lawman. He knew he had to play his cards right. He hoped Flanagan would find him first. After all, he was the more skilled gun fighter.

Horne turned and someone hit him from behind knocking him to the wet snow. His gun was kicked away and a boot turned him on his back. Vance Tillerson stood over him, pointing the barrel of his Schofield down at him.

"Time's up, Marshal." Tillerson cocked his pistol.

"Only for you," said another voice from behind Horne.

Tillerson looked up to see Jim Flanagan, both his Dragoons in his hands.

"Drop that gun and I'll spare ya," Flanagan offered.

"Hardly. You know I'll beat ya, Jim, even down one gun."

"You're fast, but can you see better in the dark?"

"Too much time in the forge has blurred your vision Flanagan, I've got ya."

"Then let's see who's really the best."

"Whenever you're ready, partner."

Both men slowly holstered their guns. They stared at one another for what seemed like an eternity. Horne watched in tense anticipation. Then, with nothing to mark the occasion other than the distant cry of an owl somewhere off in the hills, they drew. Tillerson was fast, one of the fastest draws Horne had ever witnessed. His Schofield blew thick, white smoke toward Flanagan.

But all of the quickness in the world could not save Tillerson. He was shooting the wrong target, as Horne's own gun, which he had grabbed in the confusion, discharged its last round directly at Tillerson's chest. The gunman flew backward and landed hard on the unforgiving ground. Horne let the last bit of smoke roll from his barrel before he stood up. He slid his Colt back into its holster and inspected Tillerson's body with a kick to determine the outlaw was dead.

Then he turned and saw that Flanagan was gone. No body, no blood, nothing. Then, the blacksmith appeared from the alleyway, still holding his guns. Horne figured he'd jumped behind the building when Tillerson drew, knowing Horne would draw his own gun. At least, he hoped that was the case. Either way, it was over now, and those that needed to die had done so.

"I've never been as fast as him," Flanagan confessed, holstering his Dragoons, "But sometimes, being the fastest ain't enough."

Barr came running up behind Horne, as fast as he could in his condition. He patted Horne on his shoulder, saying, "Having friends helps, too."

✪✪✪

Over the next day, the townsfolk emerged from their hidey holes and Horne filled them in on the night's events. Tillerson, his gang, and Enos were photographed, boarded up, and buried in unmarked graves on the outskirts of town. Although the ground was cold and hard, the undertaker did his job and the town's wounds began to heal.

Mayor Thomas C. Halliday's wounds healed in the jail cell of Talon's Crossing. The elders of town, including Gerwin Van Gelderen, quickly rescinded his mayorship. Later that week, the Federal Marshal came in from Carson City and took Halliday away from Talon's Crossing for the last time. Horne never received any word on his fate, but assumed it was met at the end of a noose.

Town elders announced that the mayoral election would continue as originally planned for Thanksgiving. Jim Flanagan announced his campaign would continue and no one dared run against him. He won unanimously, and was celebrated as the town's 25th mayor on Thanksgiving. He would serve for many years, doing away with any of the unjust orders of Mayor Halliday and instituting laws that worked in favor of the people of Talon's Crossing.

The men who died at the mountain pass were buried with honor and celebration in the Talon's Crossing Cemetery. With help from every member of town, the pass was cleared in one day. After that, travel to and from town returned to normal.

Deputy Seth Barr and Marshal Gideon Horne sat around the office fireplace, drinking sips of hot coffee. Barr's abdomen had fully healed and he'd earned quite the reputation as a marksman and hero among the young ladies of the Emerald Valley. Lately, he'd been courting young Alyssa Stevens, daughter of the owner of the Upward S Ranch in the western desert past town.

"You'd better be careful out there, Seth," warned Horne. "It's a woman's world once you leave the saddle."

"Sure is, Marshal. But last night I asked Mr. Stevens for Alyssa's hand."

Horne perked up, nearly spitting out his coffee. "And?"

"And he said there's no man he'd be happier having as a son-in-law."

"Congratulations!" Shouted Horne, standing up and shaking Barr's hand. Horne hesitated, and his smile disappeared.

"What's wrong, Marshal?"

"You're not leaving the office for a life of ranching, are ya, Seth?"

Barr hesitated. "No, sir, Marshal. Somebody's gotta watch your back."

"I know. That's why I was worried."

Outside, the impending snowfall of Christmas Time was quickly approaching. The skies swirled gray and blue like dirty water and created a swirling, cold wind that came down and hit the spaces between homes and buildings. Inside them, the people of Talon's Crossing were warm, well fed, and happy to have their town back to normal. Their leaders, including Marshal Horne and Mayor Flanagan, had safely guided them through another dangerous path and now they were free to return to their lives. After all, good people need good leaders, and good leaders need good people.

THE END

FOOL'S GOLD RUSH

The scope followed the mounted man across the waving green plain of the Emerald Valley. Recent fall sheds of foliage were swept across the rolling hills by a swift wind. The sky overhead, amber with envy at the setting sun, seemed to encircle the scene below like a halo. The rider stopped at the edge of a drop in the valley, which led down into the town of Talon's Crossing. He looked back and his head placed itself in the crosshairs of the scope. Then, it was over.

"Got it!" Shouted the man behind the field level, looking up from the scope. He wore a gray three-piece suit with the jacket piece missing. A gold watch chain dangled on his vest. His hair, unkempt by the strong wind of the Emerald Valley, was a flash of red against his pale, shaven face.

The mounted man galloped back to the knoll where the scope man was standing, wiping sweat from his brow. They locked eyes as the mounted rider halted his pony, a black mare, and dismounted.

"This place is lush as far as the eye can see!" Said the man near the mare, his voice revealing a feeling of glee.

"Yeah, she'll be tough to pry away from these folks," said the scope man, breathing in deeply. He continued, "But the business must roll on. You know as well as I do, Chauncey, that folks will give up anything for the almighty dollar."

Chauncey let the reins on his black mare fall loose and the animal began to graze. Chauncey was obviously the younger of the two, from the unwrinkled state of his forehead and the ever-present smile on his jaw. He wore a similar suit of faded emerald, and stood with a hand on his head, interlacing his fingers in a thick, brown mane. Neither man wore a gun.

"I guess you're right, Dave. Been that way every stop we've made this go," said Chauncey, putting his hands on his hips. He looked down into the valley toward the town. They'd passed it two days prior on their way here, but not stopped in.

"Like I said, they always do," said Dave. He was packing up his field level, scope, and other surveying accoutrements when he caught the faint sound of horses' hooves on solid soil. He lifted his head and raised up from his kneeling position, scanning the horizon.

Chauncey caught the sound, too, but long after the acute hearing of Dave had. Both men looked at one another and Chauncey made for his mare. The animal whinnied at the sudden movement of her rider but Chauncey managed to snag a rein before she could bolt. He pulled her toward him and removed a rifle from its scabbard on the saddle. It was a brand-new Winchester.

"Indians, you think?" Pondered Chauncey. His eyes wildly searched the horizon.

"Don't know," Dave replied, "Gettin' closer, though."

Suddenly, the faint sound became much more clear and gave way to a black speck on the far valley. The speck enlarged and separated into two riders, approaching fast.

"If it's the Paiute, they've dwindled in force since I last saw 'em," said Dave.

The talk of Indians irked Chauncey's spirit and he said, "You think it's the Paiute? Scalpers?"

"No, it ain't the Paiute, boy. They're long tamed. I was bustin' you." Dave watched the riders approach. Then, something caught his eye, glinting in the last rays of sunlight. He thanked his lucky stars. "Put that rifle away, Chauncey."

"What?"

Dave made a movement toward Chauncey like a father does a scolded child. Chauncey grabbed his mare and replaced the Winchester in its scabbard. Then, the riders were upon them, and it was too late to retrieve it.

"Mornin', gentlemen," said Dave. "Name's David Kemp."

"Mornin'," responded both mounted men. They looked hard-nosed and dead-set on something. The older one, with a thick mustache that covered his lips and a black hat that sat low on his brow, spit into the dirt. On his vest he wore a badge, and a pistol sat snug in its holster on his hip. The younger one, meanwhile, was spry and wiry, but his eyes showed the experience of a man double his age. He, too, wore a pistol and badge.

"How can I help you?" Asked Dave. He smiled. Chauncey was silent.

"No help needed, sir," said the older man. "Name's Gideon Horne, marshal of Talon's Crossing.

Dave swallowed and spoke, "I see. We passed the town two days past from the East. Nice looking place."

"It is," said Marshal Horne. "What are you two doin' with all this equipment?"

"Land surveyors," said Chauncey, speaking up, seemingly out of turn.

All eyes turned to him, except Horne's. His remained on Dave.

"Surveying in the Emerald Valley? For what? No companies own stake out here," said Horne.

Horne was obviously a man of intelligence, both earned and read, noted Dave. He replied, "No, sir. Not yet, at least. Me and Chauncey here are employed by the Grand Western Land Company, and they've sent us to inquire about buying up parcels in the area."

"I doubt anyone in Talon's Crossing would sell their land, mister," said the younger man, obviously Horne's deputy.

"And any part of the Valley that isn't owned ain't for sale, either," added Horne. "We like some part of our world free from the clutches of any man, Mr. Kemp."

"Understandable," said Kemp, "But the Grand Western Land Company is willing to pay double for unowned land, right into the coffers of the town itself. Maybe even a generous donation to the Marshal's Office?"

The comment rubbed Horne the wrong way. Kemp could tell through Horne's rustling mustache.

"And, if there are no parcels available out here in the Valley, perhaps some in the mountains to the west of town?" Added Kemp.

"Well, I'm not the speaker for Talon's Crossing. You're welcome to do your spiel to the townsfolk and see what answer you get. Good luck."

With that, Horne reared his mare and kicked her off toward town. The deputy was at his side every step of the way. They disappeared down the slope, leaving only the faint scent of their ponies behind them. Chauncey watched them intently, as did Kemp.

"That marshal's gonna be an impediment to our business here, Chauncey," said Kemp, in a surly voice.

"What are we gonna do?" Asked Chauncey.

"Not sure, yet," said Kemp, "But we've got an invitation to go into town, and that's enough for now."

✪✪✪

As Gideon Horne and his deputy, Seth Barr, entered the town of Talon's Crossing, they found the place empty. Horne pulled his mare up to the front of the Marshal's Office—a quaint, wooden building, but clean and well-kept—and tied her up to the hitching post. Barr followed suit.

"Well, didn't see nor hear a lick of Johns," said Barr, patting his pony on the side.

"Yeah, and unfortunate, too. Usually the Emerald Valley gives up some gems on stuff like this," Horne replied.

"You think Johns is halfway to ole Mexico by now?" asked Barr.

"No, I don't," said Horne.

"Why's that?"

"Johns seems, to me, to be the type that just can't pry himself away from an easy score. He started out a swindler, then upgraded to scamming the tracks and fights, to stealing from banks and railroad companies. He's not the type of flee easy money."

"That's a fine thought, Marshal," said Barr, "And murder, too."

"Yeah," said Horne, as he started walking away from the office.

"Where you goin'?"

"Seems dead in town," said Horne. "Gonna take this opportunity to have a drink in peace."

Horne left Barr at the Marshal's Office and walked toward the Nest. When he arrived, the general buzz from inside told him that he'd find anything but peace when he walked into the Nest. He should have known better: the Nest was the central hub in Talon's Crossing. If something happened in or around the Emerald Valley, you could bet there'd be people lined up against the bar talking about it.

As Horne stepped inside, he was greeted by a few familiar faces. Yet, most of the attention was given to a man sitting at a table in the center of the place, talking off the heads of the men around him. Upon closer inspection, Horne recognized the center of attention as Charlie Queen, the de facto real estate agent of Talon's Crossing, and the Emerald Valley as a whole. He'd arrived about five years prior and served as an intermediary between the settlers and the government. He made it his business to be fair in his dealings. Most folks liked him and many had acquired their land from him.

"So he says to me 'give me the biggest tract of land you got'," said Queen, relating his story to the men gathered around him. "I figured he was drunk or something, cause everybody around the Emerald Valley knows the Hayman's Parcel is the biggest piece of land in a hundred miles."

As Horne listened, he thought back to what he remembered about the Hayman's Parcel. In the days of the Indians wars, before the Civil War, a man named "Hayman" Brown staked a large territory in and around the Emerald Valley. Over time, he sold parts, lost parts, and gave tracts away. When he died at the outbreak of the Civil War, he left the remaining hundred acres or so to his four sons. They divided it up, but then were forced to go and fight in the war. None of them survived and the land passed into the hands of the Nevada Territory.

"But," continued Queen, after a sip of whisky, "Everybody also knows that Hayman's is one of the *worst* tracts of land in a *thousand* miles. Nobody would touch it for a buck. Full of mountainous terrain and swamp. No fertile grassland like in the Emerald Valley."

Queen was right. Hayman's lay to the west of Talon's Crossing and started the descent from lush, rolling hills to mountainous crags toward California. Nobody who had a stake in cows or property would want it. Maybe if the Jarbidge Mountains held gold or copper, but no one's ever found any trace of precious metals in those hills. Horne leaned back against the bar and watched on, tipping his hat up from his brow to get a good look at everyone around.

There was Queen at the table. He was overweight in the gut but a stocky man all over. He had a thick patch of stubble on his chin and sideburns, wearing a banker's attire of a black suit. They say bankers and real estate agents attend someone's funeral with every sale because no one can ever pay off the debt before they die. That's why they wear black.

Sitting around the table were scrawny Miles Clark, the son of Finch Clark, the tailor, burly Orin Bennett, a butcher, and Lyle Clancey, the teacher from back East. A multitude of men seemed to be enjoying Queen's story. Everyone loved news that was unique. Too often they were bogged down with marriages, deaths, births, and the occasional drunk. They yearned for the action they read about in the incoming Dodge City papers. Horne threw them away as fast as look at 'em. He knew people wanted it, but people shouldn't always get what they want, he thought.

"Poor sonovabitch," continued Queen, "He got played like a Jew harp. Sorry I had to do it to him, though. He was insistent on Hayman's Parcel."

Miles Clark spoke up, in stuttering English, "You think he found gold in 'dem hills?"

Queen and the other grown men laughed at the teenager's comments. Horne found it odd Miles wasn't in school. Even more odd that the teacher wasn't either.

"No gold in these hills," said Clancey, his teacher. His words were astute and grammatical. "Nothing but spiders and rock."

"He's right," said Orin Bennett, a native Irishman, "My poor grandad, res' his soul, said the only yello' ting he ever saw in these hills was the hair on my mamma's head."

"Either way," continued Queen, trying to get the attention back on himself. "This poor feller will be back in my office in a week, wanting his money back. A deal's a deal, though. I think you men will agree. No Indian trader's here."

They all nodded their heads in agreement, agreeing that the man deserves whatever came to him now. Just then, a thought struck Horne. He remembered the surveyors from earlier. Ketch, or Kelly, or something with a "K" was the man's name. He didn't say he'd been in town before, though. The crowd had dispersed to get drinks, urinate, and commit to other pleasures. Horne walked up to Queen and stood next to him. Queen looked up, tipping his hat to see the marshal's face.

"Ah, Marshal Horne, did you hear my story? I've sold—" began Queen.

Horne interrupted, "Heard it all, Queen. Congrats to you, sir."

Queen smiled as Horne tipped his hat.

"I was wondering," continued Horne, "If you could tell me the name of this man that bought Hayman's from you."

"Well, it's not often in the best interest of my business to be spilling my tongue wherever I go," said Queen, hardly believing himself. His goatee wriggled as he spoke.

"You spilt your tongue last month about that Brody calf you accidentally shot last spring. Hope Mr. Brody didn't hear that one," said Horne. A twinkle emanated from his eye and he almost cracked a smile at his jab.

Queen sipped on his whisky more slowly, contemplating his next move. "Ah, yes, I remember his name now. Thank you for jogging my memory, Marshal. It was Kemp... David Kemp."

There it was. The name of the man he had met earlier on his ride back into town. Kemp had claimed he never made it into town and was looking to buy on behalf of a land company. No company would ever buy a parcel of mountain, unless...

Horne left the table and walked outside. It was getting cold as the first winds of fall ripped through the barren streets of town. A woman was emptying a wash pan over the side of a railing down the way. He looked toward both ends of the street, but nothing was there. He bundled his coat around his neck, got to his mare, and headed home for some much-needed rest.

✪✪✪

A few days later, Horne rode into town in the early morning to get ready for the day. He'd spent all morning cleaning his pistol and sipping coffee. He expected he'd hear some more about Hayman's Parcel today. Deputy Barr had taken up the gossip too, and Horne couldn't keep him quiet long enough for some peace. As Horne approached the Marshal's Office, he noticed a strange horse hitched the front post. It was a palomino, uncommon in this area. Horne lost his train of thought and investigated the horse. It had all the makings of a fine horse: strong legs, nice mixture of fat and muscle. It also had the riggings belonging to a travelling man: empty scabbard, light bags, bedroll, frying pan. Horne walked up the steps and through the front door.

Inside, a man stood facing away from Horne. He was looking at the gun rack on the wall that held two rifles and a shotgun. The man was dressed in a dark overcoat, wool trousers, and thick, tall boots. With his right hand on his hip, it revealed a Spanish style holster carrying a pre-war cap and ball conversion pistol. He only knew one man who carried a pistol like that.

"Cap Crawford," said Horne.

The man turned and smiled at Horne. He was a tall man, solidly built, a few years younger than Horne. He had a thick smock of black hair and a thick, bushy mustache that covered his mouth, like Horne's. His sideburns extended down to his jaw.

Horne reached out and shook Cap's hand.

"Damn, Horne, been some time," said Cap, still smiling. His blue eyes were bright and full of excitement.

"Sure has, Cap, how long?"

"Five, maybe six years?"

"Back when you brought in the Schlosser Gang, I believe."

"You're right. That was nearly eight years now. Good to see you're still in charge around here."

Herman "Cap" Crawford was a territorial marshal employed by the Nevada Territory. Governor Adams kept a slew of marshals who patrolled the vast expanse of wilderness and settlements across the state. Cap was feared and respected wherever he went, living out of a saddle and acting as a bounty hunter with the law behind him. They'd met during a shootout with the Schlosser Gang. They'd saved each other's rears and never forgotten it.

"Yeah, the people of Talon's Crossing keep electing me, so I keep serving," said Horne.

"Always the man of the people, Horne," said Cap.

"What brings you to Talon's Crossing?"

Cap sighed and motioned for Horne to sit at the desk, as was his rightful spot. Cap pulled the chair up to the side of the desk and sat down himself. He pulled off his dusty hat and set it on the desk.

"I take it you've heard about Slick Mark Johns?"

"Of course, Barr and I've been out looking for him for the past two days. Nothing," replied Horne. He was intently watching Cap, knowing some new information would come at any moment.

"You wouldn't have. I've been tracking him Westward from the prison, been two days behind him since I started. He's fast, and sneaky, too. I doubt he's using his real name or would be recognizable."

"So," interrupted Horne, "You're here because you think he's in Talon's Crossing, possibly undercover?"

"Well, I don't know. Can't be too sure. Like I said, he's slick. Hence the name. I know he come this way."

"And didn't go too far past," said Horne, "We've been westward."

"That only leaves south and north."

"With fall in full force he wouldn't head north, I would think," said Horne.

"No, maybe not. That leaves here or south. If he headed south, the Mexicans will have their hands full and probably leave him for dead.

"Exactly why I'm here. I'm under the opinion that he wouldn't head anywhere else except here."

Horne thought back to the Nest, to the conglomerate of men surrounding Queen as he told his story. He'd meant to see every face, but only focused on those at the table, and he knew those men well. He sighed, regretting his lack of observation.

"You're the marshal here, Horne," added Cap, "And I'm here for backup, as you might call it. Another gun in case Johns is here."

"So the rumors are true? He killed that banker?"

"Very true. And his son, too. Sixteen years old. For a pile of lighted gold. Surprised he'd do it, too. Never struck me as a cold-blooded killer, based on his past convictions. Didn't fit the profile of one."

Horne remembered back to the numerous wanted flyers he'd gotten in the mail over the past few years with "Mark Johns" written across them: forgery, bribery, loan sharking, you name it. If it involved money and illegal activity, Johns was your man. Soon, the flyers read "'Slick' Mark Johns." Now, he was a runaway killer imprisoned in the West.

"The governor want him dead or back in prison?" asked Horne.

"Either way is fine with him," Cap replied. "He just wants it dealt with."

Suddenly, a commotion outside in the street caught their attention. As Horne looked up through the window, he noticed streaks of gold and orange painted across the glass from the rising sun. He could make out a few people in the street, their arms waving as they slowly formed themselves into a mass of moving, shouting faces.

Horne rose up from the desk and followed the commotion outside. Cap set his hat back on his head and followed. When Horne reached the railing of the office, he stopped and watched the commotion in the street. It wasn't the job of a town marshal to involve himself in every squabble. He'd be seen as nosy and overbearing. He'd learned to wait until his intervention was necessary.

Every one of the town folks' eyes was drawn to a team of wagons pulled by oxen that were heading down the street. The wagons were loaded down with supplies and tools. Horne couldn't make out what exactly the tools were for, but it seemed like a big operation. After the first two wagons went by the office, Horne noticed Orin Bennett, the butcher, and Lyle Clancey, the teacher from back East, talking to each other a few yards away.

"I 'tink there's some new blood comin' into Talon's Crossing," said Bennett, in his Irish accent.

Lyle Chancey spat into the dirt, "Yeah, doesn't look like they mean on throwing up a home and staying either. Looks like a business venture to my eyes."

"You wonder if it's the railroad comin' through," Bennett suggested.

"Doubt it," Chancey disagreed. "The Emerald Valley's too humpy for the tracks, I think."

"But look at 'dem Chinamen," Bennett, pointed to the next set of wagons that were coming down the street. "Aren't they da ones building the railroad?"

Horne followed Bennett's hand to the wagons and saw two wagons of nearly a dozen Chinese men in each. They looked like a rough bunch. Not troublemakers, but as if they've worked hard and lived hard most of their lives. Some wore plain suits, while others more traditional Chinese garb. A few years prior, the Transcontinental Railroad had sent a surveyor to the Emerald Valley but it turned out they were going in another direction. The folks of Talon's Crossing were a mixture of excited and regretful at the prospect of a railroad nearby. With the railroad came opportunity and money, but also people. And people, Horne knew, you couldn't always trust to be a Godsend.

The first wagon of Chinamen came by and the townsfolk eyed them up, glaring at them with distaste. Horne knew the townsfolk weren't inherently evil, but the discrimination that followed people of color in the East often intensified in the West, where people became more cautious and worrisome about protecting their own. Horne, on the other hand, had known too many well-to-do white men of good breeding who'd done wrong to judge just about anyone. He had learned, in his years as a lawman, that justice doesn't see color.

Joe Berger, a laborer for a local stock outfit, threw a clump of dirt toward the wagon and yelled a profanity toward the Chinamen. Jessie Hayes followed suit, a young man working in the stable. A couple of other men joined in the rousing of the newcomers. The Chinamen ducked their heads and looked around, cautious about where the next clump, or rock, might come from. Horne stepped down from his post and yelled out to the men to quit their horseplaying. They waved him off and walked back to their work. The fourth and last wagon passed by and continued down the street until it made it to the end of town.

"I'm gonna check this out," said Horne to Cap.

Cap nodded, replying, "I've got a date with a hot bath; see you soon."

Horne followed the wagon lines on foot out of town a ways until he saw the wagons lined up in a circular formation. He wasn't sure if it was to repel Indian or townsfolk attacks. Horne saw a white man, probably the boss of the outfit, patting down a horse with a saddle on it. He hadn't seen the man at first when the wagons came through town. Horne approached him.

"Howdy," he greeted. "Name's Gideon Horne, Marshal of this place."

The man turned and gave a gruff look of displeasure. He was bigger than Horne and muscular. A life in the saddle and mines with a shovel or pickaxe in his hand had made him so. He wore a simple faded shirt, leather breeches, and tall boots. A thick, iron Colt hung at his hip, crossdraw. He was balding, but a thick mane of golden hair clung to his face, reaching his neck.

"What the hell kind of treatment do you folks give to newcomers in the area?" Asked the man.

Horne wasn't about to excuse their actions to anyone. He even agreed with this man's assessment. "I don't doubt your treatment, sir, but I do welcome you, personally, to Talon's Crossing."

"I don't give a damn," said the man, turning back to his horse.

Horne needed information, so he continued, "You folks headed to lay track?"

"Railroad?" The man turned back. "Hell no. We're miners."

The first wagon of Chinamen came by...

"Miners? There's no mine around here."

Suddenly, two Chinamen came running toward them from town. They were carrying a man between them. As they approached, it became obvious the man was bloodied, a large slice in his forehead. One Chinaman said something to the other, who spoke up.

"This man… he hurt… by man," said the Chinaman, in broken English accented by his Chinese upbringing.

The burly man watched on intently. It was now plain he was their boss. Horne watched on.

"He try to buy… uh, flour… but no sell," said the Chinaman, thinking about each word.

The burly man turned to Horne. "This how you run your town, Marshal? Don't even let common folks buy flour to feed themselves without takin' a whoopin'?"

"No, it's not," said Horne, unable to explain it. He'd not known the townsfolk to be so standoffish and aggressive before.

"Well, they better get used to it. We have a right to be here much as the next man. We'll have barracks up in the morning, so we'll be needin' supplies. If your people don't want to sell, we'll not buy from them. We can wait."

"I think they've…" began Horne, but the burly man turned back to his horse as the Chinamen dragged off their compatriot.

Horne turned back toward town, anxious to get the scoop on what had happened. He made his way to the Nest and found a group of men there, laughing.

"What the hell happened here?" Asked Horne, in a deep voice. Everyone went quiet. It wasn't often Horne addressed them this way. "Who beat up that Chinaman?"

A man stepped forward. It was Joe Berger. Surrounding him was young Jessie Hayes, Marv Turner, the grocery man, and Edge Stevens, a cowhand.

"Joe Berger, what right have you to be whoopin' on newcomers to this town?" asked Horne.

"What right do they have bein' here?" Berger retorted? He was a well-known man in town, and quick-tempered. He was a church-going man but would have a lot to repent for each week.

"As much as anyone else," the marshal answered. "Whether we like it or not. I remember you acted similarly when Orin Bennett arrived some years ago, calling him Paddy and the like. Now it's the Chinese."

"That's different, Marshal, Bennett proved he had a right to stay here.

Found a profession and made it his own. These Chinamen, they're here for quick profit and little gain for the town."

"We don't even know who they're here for. Their bossman said they're here for mining work. There's no mines here," Horne pointed out.

Edge Stevens spoke up. "Not true, Marshal. Didn't you hear about the gold they found up on Hayman's Parcel just two days ago?"

Horne felt like he'd been gone for ages and was learning about everything that had gone on in town while he was gone. How did all of this get by his ears? And where was Seth Barr? He'd been absent on and off for the past few days.

"Who told you that?"

"Queen; said that guy that bought up the parcel came by to let him know he'd have a crew by in a few days to start hauling it all out. That's why the Chinamen are here."

Jessie Hayes butted in, "Apparently, old Hayman Brown was sittin' on a fortune."

How would Kemp know there was gold on Hayman's Parcel, thought Horne? It was all too fishy. It reeked of deceit. He grabbed Joe Berger by the arm and led him toward the door.

"What are you doin', Marshal?" Berger cried out.

"You're under arrest for assault, Joe," Horne replied and pushed him through the door.

✪✪✪

Later that night, Deputy Seth Barr stumbled in through the front door of the Marshal's Office. He looked a little drunk. Horne looked up from his desk. In the cell behind him, Joe Berger looked up from his sleep.

"Where have you been?" Asked Horne, like a father would ask an unruly child.

"Been up with that surveyor fella'," the deputy said.

The comment made Horne cringe. More of this Kemp guy? Was it not enough to lie to the people of Talon's Crossing about this gold that he had to corrupt his only deputy?

"Why?"

"Well, he approached me a few days ago and invited me up to the claim to see the gold. I figured it was all lies, as anyone would, but when I got up there he had a nugget the size of my fist!"

Horne was not one to think his own deputy a liar, nor a deceiver. But, sometimes, Barr could prove to be a little naive, as any young man could.

"You know it was gold? Gold taken out of that very ground?"

"Why would I think otherwise, Marshal?" Barr sat down at his desk and unbuttoned the top button on his shirt, freeing his neck. "Do you think this Kemp guy is no good?"

Horne thought it over. There was nothing, really, to convict Kemp on. He bought land, found gold, and now he was planning on mining it out. Had it been anyone in town, he'd be buying them a drink. Was Horne suspicious of outsiders like everyone else? What made his actions any better than that of Joe Berger, who was sitting in a jail cell?

"I don't know for sure," said Horne. "But I think it's worth more investigation. Gold is found on the oldest and largest parcel of land in the area? Don't you think it's a story too good to be true?"

Barr nodded, adding, "Sure it is, but what does Kemp have to gain?"

He wasn't sure about that yet, but he suspected something since the day he first saw Kemp. He pulled open one of his desk drawers and fumbled through some paperwork. Just as he found what he was looking for, the front door burst open. It was Cap Crawford. He had a wide-eyed look on his face.

"We've got problems," Cap announced. Horne and Barr jumped up and grabbed their hats on the way out.

Down the street, a large fire had been set to one of the makeshift tents in the "Chinese District", as the townsfolk were calling it. A slew of Chinamen were trying to stifle the blaze using their canteens, but to no avail. The fire raged on, consuming the tent and its contents. Horne hoped there were no people inside.

A gathering of townsfolk were watching the blaze from the last building in town, as if they were guarding the threshold of town. Horne, Cap, and Barr made their way over to the townsfolk.

"What's goin' on?" Horne yelled above the noise.

"Here to arrest some more of us?" Edge Stevens asked with a smirk.

"Wipe that smirk off your face," Horne cautioned. Stevens dropped his lips. "Now, somebody tell me what happened?"

Marv Turner spoke up. "I don't know who set the fire, Marshal Horne, but I can guess why." Horne doubted the first part, but needed information, so he coerced Marv with a waving hand. "Those Chinamen are bad enough, but that boss of theirs is Jim Dolittle, from the Lincoln County War down in New Mexico."

Horne knew the name well, as did everyone who read the papers.

Dolittle had been on the side of Murphy's men, but gotten out before everything went to hell. Some said he was a skilled killer, while others called him a yellow-bellied coward.

"We don't want a killer in our midst," added Edge Stevens, crossing his arms.

"You can't police everyone," said Horne. "Some folks just want to do their work and leave, you know."

"Either way," added Marv, "That's why the fire was set. I don't know who, though."

Horne left them and walked up to the Chinese District. He caught sight of Jim Dolittle, the man standing some feet above the rest. He was covered in water and dirt, obviously trying to fight the fire. When he saw Horne, he sighed.

"Marshal, you best just leave now so I don't get arrested."

"Dolittle, wait," Horne ordered. The sound of the man's name stopped him.

"How do you know my name? Is that what they told you?" Dolittle motioned to the townsfolk and started toward them.

Horne stopped him.

"Whoa, there. Hold on a second. Just hear me out, Dolittle. If I can promise you there'll be no more interference and you can get on with your work, can you promise to let me handle things?"

Dolittle thought for a moment. "I guess so. We would be out of here, normally, but there's been some hold up at the mine. Not sure when we'll start digging."

If they haven't started digging, Horne thought, where did Kemp get the first-sized nugget from? Either way, he had enough problems keeping the Chinese and the townsfolk at bay. He had other plans for Kemp. He shook Dolittle's hand, which was larger than his own, and left. On his way past the townsfolk, he stopped and glared at them.

"If any of you are caught messing with those camps and men, you'll be right next to Joe Berger, with a black eye to keep you company." The words rang true in their ears and some nodded. Horne left, and Cap and Barr followed him back.

"What are you planning to do about this?" Barr had obviously sobered up in the wake of the fire.

"Nothing. I got word from Dolittle he'll leave them be, and the townsfolk won't risk being jailed for some fun. Berger was their leader anyway, and we already have him. Seth, I want you back up at Kemp's tomorrow. Get in good with him, for I suspect he's more than meets the eye."

"What do you want to say to him?"

"Just act interested. He seems to like spreading stories, so buy into that and see what information you can get out of him."

"I think you're reading too much into the stories, Marshal. Kemp seems like a good man," Barr argued.

"I hope you're right, Seth. But I want to be sure."

With that, Barr mounted his pony and galloped out of town, leaving Horne and Cap standing in front of the Marshal's Office.

"I understand everything that's going on here," said Cap. "But we've got bigger issues. Mark Johns is laying in wait somewhere, and he's the one we should be focused on."

"I know, Cap, but I have to deal with the devil I know first. I have a feeling he'll turn up with or without me looking for him."

"You think so? I hope it ain't at the expense of an innocent life. Remember: Johns's a killer. I'm sure he'll do anything to stay out of the hangman's noose."

"I think you're right."

✪✪✪

A few days went by without any conflict. The townsfolk kept a wary eye on the Chinese District, but went about their business as usual. Dolittle and the Chinamen had set up another tent near the ashes of their old one, but were running low on supplies, having been denied by Marv Turner, the grocer. Horne didn't know how much longer they'd wait for Kemp to start mining, but if they didn't have food, he was sure they'd be on the trail to the next stop.

As Horne left the Plains Hotel, where he'd enjoyed a quiet breakfast, he noticed another commotion brewing at the east end of town. Any gathering of more than three townsfolk lately had Horne on edge. He followed the people over to Peabody's Livery & Corral at the end of the street. He followed their eyes to the pasture beyond the corral, where a sea of tents now resided. They seemed to have cropped up overnight. Some were large, multi-roomed tents, while others were small dog tents.

"Dolittle promised me no more interference," Horne mumbled aloud. "Now he's surrounding the town with his workers?"

As Horne walked toward the tents, he was stopped by Lyle Clancey, who was red-faced.

"Marshal, this is an outrage!"

"I know, Clancey. I told them not to cause any more trouble, but it looks like they have. I'll talk to Dolittle. He's the head of the Chinamen."

"This isn't the Chinamen, Marshal!" Clancey waved his hands toward the new tents. "It's freelance miners!"

Clancey explained that a slew of prospectors had arrived in the night after word had spread to the surrounding towns about Kemp's gold mine. Folks from the surrounding counties had traveled to stake their claims and cash in on the "gold rush." One miner, dirty and long-bearded, walked by Horne and Clancey. Horne spoke up and stopped the man.

"Welcome to Talon's Crossing. I'm Marshal Gideon Horne. Do you mind if I ask how you heard about this gold rush?"

The miner said that he was from Battle Mountain, a nearby town, and saw a newspaper article last week reporting that a huge gold claim was discovered in the Emerald Valley and, along with miners being needed, they suspected more strains of gold were out there. He even had a copy of the paper. It was the *Lander Times-Tribune*. Lander was the county in which Talon's Crossing had been incorporated after Nevada became a state in 1864. The article was written by David Kemp. Horne fumed inside. He was tired of Kemp's lies bringing chaos to his town. It was time to end this.

As Horne walked back to the office to mount his horse and ride out to confront Kemp, he was stopped by a sight in the alleyway between the office and Jim Flanagan's blacksmith shop. It were Edge Stevens, Jessie Hayes, and Marv Turner. They were rattling around in some backpacks. Horne suspected they were up to no good.

"What are you doin' over there?" Horne asked forcefully.

The trio turned around and tried to hide what they were doing. Horne pushed through them and looked at the gear lying on the ground. There were three backpacks, various camp items, and some axes and pans. It was mining gear.

"In the prospecting business now, gentlemen?"

"We got a good deal on it," said Turner.

"Yeah, some miner keeled over last night and his brother sold his stuff to us for a good price," Stevens elaborated.

"After all the hell you gave those Chinamen, now you're fraternizing with the miners and going to stake your own claim?"

"Don't judge us, Marshal, we're just trying to get ours before the outsiders do," said Turner.

"Are you selling supplies to the miners?" Horne inquired.

Turner did not respond, as his answer was obvious. Young Jessie Hayes began packing his bag again.

"Does your old man know where you're at?" The marshal asked.

Jessie did not reply.

"Don't badger him, Marshal, he's just smarter than you," said Stevens. "He knows us folk of Talon's Crossing deserve that gold more than anybody else. We're heading out tonight."

"That mountain pass is as unforgiving as a rattler at night, Stevens," Horne reminded them. "You all know that."

"Yeah, but those miners will beat us if we wait until the morning. We know the paths. We can do it." Stevens said undeterred.

Horne turned and left. They'd made their bed, now they'd lie in it. He had bigger issues to deal with than some stupid townsfolk. As he went back to his horse, he saw Gerwin Van Gelderen, proprietor of the Plains Hotel, standing outside, smiling. He had his hands on his hips. Gerwin was Horne's age, his pale skin and frail frame made him look older. He wore a black suit and tie, with a silver watch chain on the vest.

"What are you smiling about, Gerwin?" They were good friends, and he felt he could speak plainly with him.

"I am making a killing off of these newcomers," Gerwin chuckled. "I've never had the whole place booked before. Two days straight now!"

"That's good, I guess." Horne regretted not thinking of the economic boom this might give the town, real gold rush or not.

"Mattias said he's been busy all day long with work and Peabody told me he's got one horse left!" Mattias was the launderer and Peabody owned the stable and corral. Horne figured the Nest was making a killing, too. Anywhere that served liquor was likely to see a nice profit with thirsty miners around.

"Well, good luck to ya. Hope you get yours while it lasts."

"Do you mean the gold will dry up?"

"I mean I don't think there's gold at all," Horne clarified. The comment made Gerwin's smile disappear. "Just be ready for things to return to normal soon. Don't go around throwing cash everywhere like it'll be profits forever."

Gerwin nodded, adding, "Thank you, Gideon. I can always count on the truth from you."

"Keep an eye out for some scuffles, too. These kinds of folks are bound to clash when put in the same town."

With that, Horne rushed out of town toward Hayman's Parcel. On his way there, he noticed a slew of newcomers making their way into town, braving the perilous mountain passes as they did. Folks needed to get to town before they went prospecting for supplies and rest. It was unlikely any of them had the man or horsepower to make a full trek from home to the wilds to prospect, unless they were skilled and experienced.

✪✪✪

It took Horne a good hour to get to Hayman's Parcel from town. He galloped at a steady speed, never overloading his mare. He called her Penny, for her copper color, and she'd been with him for years now. A good, well-mannered horse deserved the respect of a brisk but steady pace. He only ran her hard in an emergency.

When he arrived, he saw a small outcropping of tents in the distance. The land here was rocky and barren of good, fertile soil. The trees here were big pines, and barren from strong winds at this altitude. Horne rode up to the tents, but no one was there. He looked around a bit, being careful not to overstep his bounds. Even as a lawman, trespassing could get you shot. He saw a few mining tools, but nothing like a full-scale operation would need. He also saw pen and paper set out on a field desk. He thought back to Kemp's article in the paper. He fumed again, but did not let it show. Suddenly, horses sounded in the valley below.

Horne stepped away from the tent, closer to his horse. He saw three riders. It was Kemp, the boy who rode with him, and Barr. They were smiling and talking, until they saw Horne. Kemp rode up and faked a smile.

"Hello, Marshal," Kemp smiled.

"Howdy," replied Horne.

"What brings you out here? Come to fetch your deputy? 'Nother to-do in town?"

"No, sir, towns' doing great. All your publicity has brought in lots of good business," said Horne.

The comment caught Kemp off-guard. It was obvious that Kemp and Horne had something stuck between them, but neither could wholly place it. Kemp lost his smile for a second, but then it returned, showing his white teeth.

"Good to hear. I hoped it would accomplish that when I wrote the article," replied Kemp.

"Barr, we got a prisoner needs feeding down at the jail," said Horne.

"What brings you out here? Come to fetch your deputy?"

Barr nodded and walked his pony away from Kemp and the boy.

"Good to see you again, Seth, come back anytime," said Kemp.

"Yeah, Seth," added Chauncey, "See ya soon." He smiled.

"Wanna take a look around, Marshal, see what's bringing in the business?" Kemp invited Horne, smirking.

"Sure," Horne nodded. The comment surprised everyone, especially Kemp. Horne was not usually one to put himself in the frying pan, but he wanted to prove he was right about Kemp. He knew there was no gold mine, but Kemp had underestimated him with the comment.

"Okay, Marshal, come on." Kemp turned his horse back the way he had come. "Chauncey, get dinner started up for when I get back. The good Marshal and I will be back soon."

Barr and Chauncey watched as Horne and Kemp disappeared down a rocky pass in the mountain. Horne looked back one time, locking eyes with Barr, wondering what would have changed by the time he saw him next. If he saw him again at all?

As they rounded a pass in the trail, they found themselves entirely alone, surrounded by Nature and her creations. It was quiet, though, no birds chirping, no wind blowing. Just silence. Horne looked ahead of him, at Kemp, who led his stud in silent reprieve. He wore the same suit as before, and had no visible weapon on him, neither pistol nor rifle.

Suddenly, Kemp took a turn and left the trail. He led his stud down a deep slope of rocky outcroppings. The horse struggled to get through the briars and sharp rocks, but Kemp led him nonetheless.

"Where you goin'?" Horne spoke up.

"You don't think there'd be a trail that leads right to the gold, do you, Marshal?"

It made sense. Had there been a trail, the gold would have been discovered long ago. Horne decided to follow him down, as best he could. His mare whinnied at the first rock that scraped her sides and hesitated in the path made by Kemp's stud. He gave her a nudge and a confident remark and she followed. She was confident in Horne's leadership, which made all the difference.

As he guided his mare down the gulch, Horne had lost sight of Kemp ahead of him. He and his horse reached a flat surface on the side of the mountain, where it changed into a dense thicket of pines. Between the slope and the thicket was a narrow ledge in the mountain. Horne looked down into the ravine, and it fell deep into the heart of the mountain. It was wide enough for a man or two to fit inside, not that anyone would want to. He kicked his mare and she gracefully jumped the gap. Horne looked around, but Kemp was gone. He couldn't hear any sign of horse nor rider. He fingered the hammer loop on his pistol and removed it, preparing for a surprise attack. Suddenly, Kemp appeared on his right, from behind a bushy Pinyon pine.

"Right over here, Marshal," he said.

Horne let go of his pistol and placed his hand nonchalantly on his hip. "Quite a trail, Kemp."

"Yeah, it is, but worth it."

He followed Kemp through the pines and it opened up into the belly of the gulch, where a stream flowed down the slope of the mountain. Kemp dismounted and reached down to grab a drink of fresh, cool water. His animal did the same.

"Meant to say, fine mare you got."

"Yeah." Horne agreed dismounting. "She is. Been faithful and obedient all her life."

"Strong, too, by the looks of her." Kemp patted his stallion on the flank. "I've always preferred the studs, myself. Sure, they're a bit ornery and like to have it their way, but when the time comes for running, they'll beat any mare out there."

"No doubt. It's just nature. So where's this gold?"

"Well, it's here." Kemp pointed down into the water where he crouched.

Horne had been kneeling to get a drink, and now looked past the water's edge and into the stream. It wasn't three feet wide nor two feet deep, but it sparkled from the large nuggets of gold that sprinkled the sediment at the bottom. It reflected the sun that tipped over the peak of a large pine and hit Horne in his face. He shook his head, unable to believe what he was seeing. He reached down, picked up a thumb-sized piece, and stared at it.

"You were right," he muttered under his breath.

"Of course I was," Kemp boasted. "I'm not a plain liar, Marshal Horne."

Suddenly, a click sounded next to Horne's head. He turned and, out of his right eye, caught sight of a small Derringer pointed at his head. It had been nestled in Kemp's left jacket sleeve with some metal contraption. He'd seen them on gamblers and the like. Horne didn't move, realizing his mistake. He thought Kemp was a swindler, but actually, he was a killer. He wouldn't make that mistake again. Horne slipped the gold nugget in his vest pocket.

"Get up," Kemp ordered ,pointing the Derringer at Horne and motioning toward a pine tree. "And pick a tree to die next to."

"Why kill me?"

"You've been like a bloodhound on my trail since I got here, and I aim to make one less burden in this burdensome place. Sending that deputy was all I could handle. Damn kid asks more questions than you do."

"If you've done nothing wrong, why worry?"

Kemp snickered. "Don't you know who I am?"

Horne looked at the man in front of him. He was tall, fairly slim, and well-dressed. He had a ruggedly handsome face and, under his hat, Horne could make out thick, red locks. He remembered the flyer in his desk drawer and what it described: "tall, lean, good-looking man with bright orange hair…. 'Slick' Mark Johns."

"Mark Johns," Horne finally realized.

"Very good, Marshal," said the fugitive. "Very good, indeed. You're smart. I knew it from the second I saw you in the valley. I knew you would be the one I needed to watch out for. And now, I'm dealing with my problems."

As Kemp moved to fire, a yell rang out in the pine grove. Kemp hesitated. The shout rang out again. "Marshal!" "Marshal Horne!" It was Seth Barr's voice, carrying down the gulch and through the grove. He would never make it in time.

Horne dove at Kemp and tackled him to the ground. The Derringer did not fall from his hands, as it was lodged tightly in its metal holster. Kemp threw the arm at Horne and it hit him in the head. The metal contraption slashed his forehead and he was thrown backwards. Horne didn't hesitate to think, just moved. He ran, dodging between pines. A shot rang out, catching him in the right arm and sending a shock of searing pain through his right side. He ran more, moving side to side, behind pines, under overhangs.

Horne saw the slope ahead and, if he could ascend it, he'd be with Barr, who was carrying his pistol and rifle. They'd have Johns dead to rights. He jumped the gap in the rock and tried to latch onto a rock ledge. He winced in pain from his right shoulder and grabbed the rock with his left hand. If he fell, he'd fall into the rock crevice, likely to his death. The movement to his left hand had turned him around. He saw Johns approaching, derringer in hand. Johns pointed it at the Marshal and fired. Horne's grip broke and he slid from the boulder. He kicked his legs as he slid, sensing the abyss was swallowing him. Then, he was gone.

✪✪✪

Seth Barr looked toward the pine forest to the east. He'd heard the gunshot, and was holding his pistol at the ready. His horse was whinnying and stamping the hard-packed dirt. Barr knew Horne and Kemp had descended into the gulch, but he didn't know what had happened inside. He suspected Kemp was a swindler, but a killer? Unlikely. In the time he'd spent with him, Kemp had been an overly nice to Barr, obviously aware he was sent by Horne to spy on him.

Suddenly, a man appeared on the path. He was on horseback; it was Kemp. There was no gun on him that Barr could see. He didn't suspect he'd been the shooter. He looked past him as his stud ascended the slope, but Marshal Horne was gone.

"Where's Marshal Horne?"

Kemp made it to the flat surface of the rocky trail. His horse was breathing heavily from the climb. Kemp hesitated. Finally, he mustered a story, "We were down in the gulley and someone started shootin' at us. I saw Horne shot in the back."

"No," gasped Barr, his lips parting in disbelief.

"We made a run for it. Horne fell back some. Another shot. Then he was down. I didn't stop running till I got to my horse. It must have been someone good with a gun who was shooting, because every shot seem to hit its mark."

Barr made a movement toward the ravine. Kemp held out a hand to stop him. "There's no use, Seth. I saw him go down with two gunshots. There's a killer in there. We need more guns."

"All respect, sir, but you don't know Marshal Gideon Horne," Barr said as he pushed past Kemp and descended into the ravine.

In the gulch, Seth Barr looked past every tree, under every low-hanging branch, and behind every rock large enough to conceal a man Horne's size. He knew he was alive. He could feel it. Men who worked together for long enough got that way. If he was dead, he'd know it. Barr kept his finger on the trigger of his pistol the entire time, aware of the killer that might still lurk in the shadows. If he shot at a lawman, he'd not care about his deputy, either.

Barr walked through the pine grove and looked down into the ravine that separated the grove from the slope, pulling Horne's mare behind him. If he'd fallen in, there was likely no way he'd get out now. Especially if he was shot twice, like Kemp said. Barr hollered down into the crevice, but there was no response. It was possible, thought Barr, that the killer took him hostage. Indians often did that. So did men who wanted a ransom. He couldn't think of anyone who'd want him dead, aside from an old enemy.

With a sigh of regret, Barr mounted his horse and kicked her up the slope, Horne's mare following closely behind. Barr felt as if he'd let his boss down by not coming to his aide. He hoped it wasn't too late. The horses steadily climbed the slope and disappeared back up onto the trail.

✪✪✪

In the darkness of the crevice, Marshal Gideon Horse lay prone on his back. His body was mangled and his clothes torn. He was bleeding from various spots, and would surely have been dead if not for a strong build and a stroke of luck. Slowly, Horne's eyes opened. He blinked numerous times, staring up at the faint light that permeated the top of the crevice. He was surrounded by darkness at the bottom.

Horne remembered the shots from Kemp. The running. The fall. He moved his right hand to grab his gun. It was still in the holster. He sighed, groaning like an injured animal. He couldn't move his shoulder without intense pain. He rolled onto his left side and tried to get up, but couldn't. He was sore all over. He breathed deeply, exhaling and pushing soft dust against the rocky crevice wall. It was a tight squeeze. Only enough room to sit up at most.

Horne thought about Kemp. He fumed more than ever, wanting to see him dead. He pushed the thoughts away, knowing they could not help him now. Anger would cloud his judgment. No, right now he needed a purpose. He thought about Barr, about Cap, and the townsfolk. All the people who would be unaware of Kemp's true identity as Slick Mark Johns, the swindler; the killer—his attempted killer. He used all his strength to lift himself with his left arm and got into a seated position.

Horne looked up, staring at the sunlight longingly. If only he had a rope. He reached out with his right arm and, despite the searing pain in his upper shoulder, he pushed through it and grabbed onto the rock wall beside him. He grabbed with his left arm and used it to lift most of his weight. Suddenly, he fell to his knees. He breathed in deeply, then out again. He was exhausted from the threat on his life and now he had to fight for it again. If he didn't, not only might he perish, but his friends would, too.

Horne gritted his teeth and lifted himself up again. He looked down once more to see if anything had dropped from his gunbelt, but all was still intact. His hat was gone, but was likely at the top, where Kemp had chased him. He grabbed the rock walls and lifted himself up, raising his legs to climb. The first ten feet were simple enough: right arm, right leg, left arm, left leg. Then, he started to feel the stretching of ligaments and muscles in his legs. His arms started to burn. He was nearly halfway, but he doubted if he could go any farther.

Seth Barr's face came to mind. The slim, young deputy who had saved his skin numerous times. He would be a good marshal, if Horne perished. He climbed. He pushed the bad thoughts away. He thought of Gerwin, of Gerwin's family. No more pork and taters for breakfast. He climbed. He thought of Jim Flanagan, the mayor and blacksmith, and the good he'd done since Horne helped him get elected. He climbed.

Soon, he was near the top. He could feel a slight breeze from the clear air above. He'd heard the sound of his own panting for what seemed like ages now. He looked up, then back down. He was nearly fifty feet high, he guessed. A fall now might kill him. Suddenly, his palms began to sweat and knees began to shake. He focused on the climb, on his friends, and, to get the last foot necessary, of revenge on Slick Mark Johns.

Horne lay on the flat stone beside the crevice, heavily breathing and sweating like a chipper stud. He lay on his back and stared up at the sun. It was afternoon now, and Johns was already back in Talon's Crossing, he guessed. Horne would see him again, he knew that much. That was all he needed.

"Where's my horse?" He asked, looking around.

Deputy Seth Barr, David Kemp, and Chauncey arrived on horseback in Talon's Crossing about two o'clock. As they rode in, they made straight for the Marshal's Office at Barr's behest. Suddenly, however, they ran into Cap Crawford, who was standing between a rugged-looking miner and Gerwin Van Gelderen.

"You owe me money, you stinking miner!" Shouted Gerwin. "I don't owe you squat!" The old man protested.

"Whoa, whoa, whoa!" Shouted Crawford. "Hold on!"

"I let you stay two nights without pay and now you say you don't have the money!" Shouted Gerwin, again. The miner got close to him and Gerwin pushed him backward.

In the ruckus, Cap sighed and looked around when he noticed the three riders approaching. "Where the hell have you been?" Cap pointed at Barr.

"Horne is hurt," Barr exclaimed. "We gotta go back out there." He explained to Cap what had happened, and that there was a killer on the loose.

"I understand, but we've got chaos here, too." Cap hesitated. "The townsfolk and miners are at war, and meanwhile the Chinese are stealing supplies and want revenge for their tent. Horne would want us to deal with this first."

Barr sighed. Inside, he agreed. If only Horne was here. Suddenly, Kemp rode forward.

"Look, men, we've got to get this town in order. Barr, if you don't mind me takin' the lead here, but I've had dealings with this kind of stuff in the land business before. Cap, you seem to be the best to talk with the Chinese and their boss, Dolittle. Go and see if you can get what they want as recompense. Barr, you know the townsfolk well. Talk to them over at the saloon and try to make them see that these miners won't be here forever. I'll go speak with the miners. Chauncey, come with me."

With that, Kemp and Chauncey rode away toward the corral and the miner's camp.

"Man, that's one assertive land agent," said Cap.

"Yeah, he seems to know what he wants, that's for sure," Barr concurred. "I don't like leaving Horne out there somewhere, all alone."

"I know, but he's right about what we gotta do. Horne is strong, Seth, you know that. If he made it out, he'll make it back."

✪✪✪

Horne dragged himself down the trail. His tired legs scraped briars and bushes, overgrown weeds, and jagged rock edge. He'd passed Kemp's camp some time before, but found it cleared of all supplies. Johns was probably on the run now. He hoped Barr had made it out and took his mare, too. He passed a fork in the trail and followed the steep, rocky path back toward town.

Then he heard yelling. Someone was making a lot of noise, scrambling up or down the path. Horne threw his body into a divot in the rock wall to his right and hid himself behind a bent pine sapling. He listened to the commotion.

"Grab the ledge! Right there! Grab it!" Horne thought he recognized the voice.

"I...can't...reach it!" Hollered another voice.

"He's goin' down."

"Don't say that, you dimwit!"

Horne knew who it was now. He pulled himself out of the divot and hobbled down the path. Sure enough, ten yards away, was Edge Stevens and Jessie Hayes. They were looking over the edge of the trail, where it fell into a very angled slope that no man nor beast would want to fall into. Horne chuckled at it now, having fallen where he did. He walked up behind them and Jessie turned. He jumped back in shock.

"Marshal!"

Edge Stevens turned and looked the lawman up and down. "Marshal... what happened to you?"

"Ran into some trouble," Horne answered curtly. "What's the issue here?" He peered over the edge.

Marv Turner was hanging onto the ledge, his backpack stuck against the rock wall, being punctured by a stick. It kept him from climbing up. Down further on the slope lay a dead horse.

"Help me, Marshal," Marv cried upon seeing him.

"Well, Marv, it looks like you should've taken my advice."

"I know it," mumbled Marv.

"We all do," added Stevens. Jessie nodded.

"If I help you boys outta this jam, promise me you'll give me a hand when I get back to town?"

They all nodded.

"Now, Marv, you need to cut that backpack free. You got a knife?"

"No, I don't."

Horne pulled a stag-handled knife from the back of his belt and readied to drop it down to Marv. The man squirmed.

"Don't!" he shouted.

"You gotta catch it by the handle, Marv, or you'll cut your hand," warned Horne.

"I can't!"

"Yes, you can. Because if you don't, you'll drop my good knife and I'll be riled. You don't want that, do you?"

"No, sir, I suppose not." With that, Horne let the knife drop, handle first, and Marv awkwardly managed to snag it midair. He smiled and they all cheered for him. After cutting himself free from the backpack, Marv climbed up easily and was reunited with his friends.

"Thank you, Marshal," Marv said while catching his breath. "I owe you my life."

"Well, you keep your life. I just need a good gun hand."

With that, they all mounted the remaining two horses, doubling up, and lit out for Talon's Crossing. On the way, Horne filled them in on who David Kemp truly was, what happened, and what he planned to do when he got to town. Although he could sense they were afraid, they showed courage. He hoped that'd be true when bullets started flying.

✪✪✪

In Talon's Crossing, Seth Barr had just finished speaking with Queen, Mayor Flanagan, and some others at the Nest when he walked out into the street. Although it took some coercion, they'd agreed to bide their time until the "rush" ended and the newcomers would leave. He'd bought time before an all-out war began.

In the street, he caught sight of Cap Crawford heading the same way, followed by Jim Dolittle and his Chinamen. Behind Barr, the town folks stepped out of the doors of the Nest and watched them.

Cap spoke first, "Dolittle agrees that there's been too much tension. The Chinamen are angry at losing the tent, but agree that the goods stolen were worth more than an old tent anyways. If the folks of Talon's Crossing will call it square, they'll leave them alone and move on at the end of the week. Kemp hasn't paid up and they've got work in California, anyway."

"Good," said Mayor Flanagan, "then consider it square."

Doolittle stepped forward, a big, burly man. He wore a pistol on his hip. He spoke to Flanagan, "I apologize for what they've done. I try to talk them down, but they're proud people, like you folks. I can only do my best here."

"Same here," said Flanagan.

From down the other way came a group of miners. They were carrying rifles with them, along with clubs, or shovels, or pickaxes. Kemp and Chauncey were not leading them. Barr looked around for the duo.

"We heard you folks been spoutin' off about us," said one of the miners. It was the same old man that had tangled with Gerwin earlier.

The townsfolk looked confused, as did Doolittle. Barr spoke up, "What do you mean? Sure, we've had our differences, but like Kemp probably told you, we want peace."

"Peace?" The old timer laughed, as did some of his followers. There were a dozen or more. "Peace? Kemp said you planned on runnin' us outta town tonight, maybe even lynching a few of us for claim-jumpin'."

"None of us thought that," declared Mayor Flanagan. He stepped

Doolittle stepped forward...

forward, in a defensive way, to protect his people.

"And you," said the miner to Dolittle and the Chinamen. "Kemp said you all planned to rob us blind, you bunch of slanty eyed foreigners!"

The miner tried to swing the pickaxe at one of the Chinamen, but Dolittle blocked it and hit the old man square in the jaw. The miner fell back to the ground, knocked out cold. The miners rushed Dolittle and swarmed him with blows. Flanagan and the townsfolk came to his aide, seeing him as an ally now. Only Cap and Barr kept their distance, unsure what to do.

Flanagan knocked down one of the miners, a tall and lanky fella, but was struck by the back end of a shovel from a close ally. Gerwin Van Gelderen suddenly dove into the fray with a frying pan, swinging it wildly at the Chinamen, at the miners, and even the townsfolk. Suddenly, a gunshot rang out. The crowd of fighting men stopped and went silent. All eyes followed the sound to a man that stood at the edge of town, near the Chinese District. He was haloed by three others, on horseback.

"Is that—?" Asked Cap, his hat having been knocked off and hair in a mess.

"Marshal Horne!" shouted Barr. He ran to the end of the street and caught Horne just as his legs gave out.

"He found us in the mountain pass," said Edge Stevens.

"And he saved my life, too," blurted Marv Turner.

"Thank God you're okay." Barr held up his mentor using his shoulder. He walked him gently over to the porch at the Marshal's Office and set him down.

"Where were you?"

"Between a rock and a hard place," Horne smirked. He explained what'd happened and how he got out. The three groups—townsfolk, Chinamen, and miners—all listened intently. Soon, it became clear who the cause of all their angst and confusion was: David Kemp, alias Slick Mark Johns. For some reason, however, Horne kept Kemp's alias a secret, playing his cards close to his vest. He didn't want anyone knowing how dangerous this man was, exactly.

"Let's string him up!" Shouted one of the miners.

"Back in the ole' country," said Orin Bennett, "We'd tie 'em up to the back of a wagon and drag him down Main Street."

"I like that idea!" shouted one of the Chinamen.

"Nice to see everybody working together," Barr commentated wryly.

Cap Crawford spoke up. "Look, we gotta make sure Kemp is stopped.

He's a killer, a cold-blooded one. He's making his way to Mexico or Canada or God-knows-where by now."

"He's right," Marshal Horne groaned. "We need to split up and make the most of our numbers. Dolittle and your workers, you guys head west to the mountains. You're the least supplied and I doubt he'd go back the way he came. You mining men, take the north route. It's cold that way and Johns is a southern man, but you never know. Then, Mayor Flanagan and the townsfolk, you go east. He said he'd come from that direction as he passed town, so maybe he's got supplies stashed. Me, Cap, and Barr will go south. He was scouting the land out there when we first saw him, so maybe we'll get lucky."

Everyone disembarked except for Horne, Barr, and Cap. The miners got on their mules and wagons, the Chinamen on the oxen-led teams, and the townsfolk on what horses they could scavenge. Flanagan gave a tip of his hat to Horne as they left eastward from town. When the three lawmen were left alone, Cap spoke up.

"You really think any of those groups can catch him?"

"No. I doubt they can provide much assistance if a gunfight breaks out. Not sure any of them have held a pistol on a man before."

Horne pushed himself up from the porch where he sat. He was still in pain. "No, I know Kemp is not going anywhere but south. That's why we're goin' south."

"How do you know that?" Deputy Barr was confused.

"Kemp isn't his real name. He's actually Slick Mark Johns."

"The runaway outlaw? What the hell is he doing here?"

"Probably tryin' to make some quick cash on this gold rush, maybe even rob some folks on his way out."

"Way out where?"

"South, like I said. He wouldn't go west, cause its the mountains and he ain't too familiar with this land. Not north, because the newspaper Kemps' article was in mentioned the 7th Cavalry was headed south on an excursion. Not east because he don't wanna go back to prison. Nope, south is it for Johns."

"Fine reasoning, Marshal," said a voice from beside the Marshal's Office.

All three lawman turned. It was Slick Mark Johns. Only now, he had no hat covering his fiery orange locks and was holding a Colt in his hands, likely a .32 caliber, from the looks of it. Cap was the only lawman who drew, but he shouldn't have. Johns motioned to Chauncey, who was across the street, perched on the porch of the Nest, his Winchester pointed at them.

Horne spoke up. "Cap, put it away. We're at a disadvantage here."

Johns laughed. "You're right about that, Marshal."

Horne felt Cap's pistol dig into his side. He craned his neck and looked down at the large revolver pointed at his abdomen. He shook his head.

"How long you been working with Johns?" he asked his old friend.

Cap's face was all seriousness. "Since before we got here, unfortunately for you."

"Where'd you hide?" Seth Barr wanted to know.

"In the only spot I knew you two wouldn't look," Johns laughed.

Suddenly, Joe Berger stumbled out of the Marshal's Office door, rubbing his eyes as if he'd just awakened.

"Door was opened, figured I'd been released."

"Not yet, mister," said Cap, motioning him back inside with his pistol. Berger slowly backed up into the office and shut the door behind him.

"So, you hide in my own jail and now you plan to kill me?" Horne wouldn't show any fear. It wasn't in him. "For what?"

"Gold, you dimwit. I showed you the river; it's teeming with it."

"And you were gonna split it with ole Cap Crawford here, if he helped you?"

Cap nodded. "I know it looks bad to you now, Horne, but the cost of living is goin' up. Our way of life is fading. I need a retirement plan. Johns offered one better."

"I thought we were friends," Horne glared at him.

"We are, and that's why I just didn't gun you down from the beginning. I tried to make things work in town, make folks get used to the idea of newcomers and of economic boom. But you just had to stick your neck in everything we done."

"Well, when someone is planning dubious things, in my town, that's my job."

"Not anymore," said Johns. "After you two are gone, Cap Crawford will be marshal of Talon's Crossing. He'll usher in a new era of prosperity for this valley."

"Yeah?" Horne questioned. "Cause you've already seen how that worked out."

"People will fight," Cap opined. "It's the way of things. They need a level head and open mind to help them see things straight."

"Good luck," said Horne.

"Get 'em on their knees," Johns commanded. "We don't have all day. Those folks will be back soon. We gotta get 'em dead and make it look like they are the real criminals."

Cap pushed Horne to the ground and Barr did it on his own. Cap pointed his pistol at Horne's head, but hesitated. Johns did the same to Barr, but looked intent. Without notice, Joe Berger burst through the door behind them, firing a double-barrel shotgun in their direction. The first shot hit the railing right behind Cap and Johns. Both men ducked, allowing Horne and Barr to push them backward and escape to cover.

The fleeing lawmen ran to the opposite side of the Marshal's Office. Chauncey had begun to fire his Winchester from the porch across the street, but didn't hit anything. When Horne reached cover, he pulled his pistol and checked the cylinder. A full six rounds. Barr was loaded, too. On the porch, Berger had unloaded the last of the buckshot and dove back inside the Marshal's Office.

Horne whispered to Barr, "I'm goin' around back, you stay here and cover the front. If you see Berger, tell him to get loaded and use the side window to fire from."

Barr nodded and Horne took off around the back. He led with his gunhand, the nickel-plated pistol catching some rays of sunlight that bent around Miss Fink's Restaurant. He jumped around the back corner of the Marshal's Office and expected to see an armed man, but none was there. Suddenly, shots were fired from the front of the building, in the street. It was a pistol, then another, and finally a Winchester broke in.

Horne used the gunplay to his advantage and ran around the other side of the building. He caught sight of Cap Crawford firing from behind the porch at Seth Barr, who was not visible. Horne had him dead to rights, raised his pistol, and "bang!"

A gunshot rang out, nearly hitting Horne in the head. The bullet lodged itself in the side of the Marshal's Office. Horne ducked and pointed his pistol to his left, where Mark Johns was firing at him from behind the blacksmith's shop. Horne fired back, nearly winging Johns in the leg. The outlaw dove behind a barrel at the rear of the building.

The shooting turned Cap's attention to Horne, who was prone on his knee. Cap fired at him once, missing. Suddenly, the window of the Marshal's Office was burst open by the barrel of a shotgun and Joe Berger unloaded a spray of buckshot right at Cap Crawford. It threw Crawford back against the wall of Flanagan's blacksmith shop, where he fell to the dirt and screamed out in pain.

Chauncey had run across the street and was firing his Winchester at Barr, who was still on the opposite side of the Marshal's Office porch. Berger aimed his shotgun at Chauncey and fired again, but the buckshot spray was ineffective at long range. Chauncey turned to run toward the alley between the blacksmith and the next building.

Horne, meanwhile, had moved to the wall of Flanagan's shop and waited on Johns to make his move. He could hear rustling behind the barrel. Cap Crawford had gone quiet, but movement turned Horne's head back to the street. He caught sight of Seth Barr walking slowly past the alleyway. He nodded to Horne, who returned the nod. Joe Berger was out of sight.

Horne knew he had to make a move before Chauncey made his way back to Johns. Teamed up, it'd be hard to penetrate their defenses. Horne turned and aimed at the barrel. Nothing. Leading with his pistol, he slowly walked around the barrel until he cleared it. Johns was gone. He looked left, then right, but nothing. Suddenly, a scraping above his head led his eyes to Mark Johns, perched on top of the blacksmith building, pistol aimed at Horne.

Horne dove forward as the first blast rang out. It caught his boot and he smashed into the back of the building. Chauncey emerged from beside the building and tried to fire at Horne, but Barr arrived from the opposite side and fired, hitting Chauncey in the chest with a bullet. Chauncey fell back dead, his gun still in his hand.

Johns fired at Barr, who ducked back behind the Marshal's Office. Johns slid to his left, but Joe Berger was sticking out of the window again and let loose with both sides of the shotgun. The shot either hit Johns or scared him, as he fell backward over the slant of the roof and rolled down and off the front of the blacksmith's shop.

Horne heard the commotion and ran down the alley toward the front of the building. He heard Barr following down the other alley. When Horne got to the street, he saw no sign of Johns. He looked left, then right, and saw a man running toward the public corrals. Barr took off after him, but Horne could not keep up, his body sore all over.

Horne watched as Barr made it to the front of the livery barn. A horse came running out of the barn and Johns was on its back, kicking it as hard as he could. Barr was narrowly missed, and fired three shots that went wide of Johns. As Johns rode westward down the street, Horne raised his pistol, aimed and pulled the trigger. It was empty.

Johns sped past him toward the Chinese District. Suddenly, he reined his horse and came to a halt in the center of the street. Horne looked past Johns, and saw the troupe of Chinamen on their oxen-led wagons, Dolittle leading them on horseback. They were headed toward town.

Johns reined his pony and turned back, riding back down the street.

Horne turned and saw the miners coming down the slope to the north of town, coming slow on horseback. Johns caught them in his sight, too, and kept riding eastwardly. There, Barr waited, but did not fire. Behind Barr, a slew of townsfolk was ascending the crest of a hill from the east. Johns reined the horse again and slid to a stop. Barr aimed and fired another shot, but it was high and to the right. The attempt forced Johns to move. He blew past Horne, who was still standing in front of the Marshal's Office, and kept riding hard. This time south.

Horne climbed up the stairs to the Marshal's Office porch. Joe Berger appeared, shotgun in hand, but Horne pushed past him. He ran to a back closet of the office and pulled out a long piece of hard leather. He laid it on the table as Barr appeared in the door. Horne untied three rawhide straps and opened the leather case. Inside was something wrapped in canvas.

"He's gettin' away to the south, Marshal," Barr stated the obvious. "I missed four times."

Horne replied, "We only need one good shot."

"No one can make a shot as far as he is now," said Berger, who had been looking for Johns out the broken window.

Horne pulled back the canvas and revealed a .52 caliber Sharps rifle with attached brass scope. It was highly polished and well-cared for. Horne opened a small box that was set inside and pulled out a single, large cartridge. He pulled out the rifle, loaded it, and walked outside. In the far distance, he could see a mounted rider still heading south. Horne motioned for Barr to come over.

"Get on one knee and let me use your shoulder. I can't hold it up with this bullet in my shoulder." He still had the Derringer slug in his arm. Barr dropped to one knee. Horne lifted the big rifle onto his deputy's left shoulder. Barr plugged his left ear with a finger, leaving his right open.

Horne knelt behind Barr. He let out a sigh and felt his heart start to slow down. He let all other noises fade out, including the murmurs of the people who had gathered behind him. He felt the trigger, the stock on his shoulder, and then looked down the scope with his open right eye. He centered it on the rider in the distance, probably over a quarter of a mile away. He let his left eye open, too, then squeezed the trigger. A shot rang out, loud and deep. After a delay, Horne looked down the scope and saw a riderless horse galloping in the distance.

When Horne lifted his head and turned back, a group of people had gathered and now joined in a ceremonious clapping. He smiled, stood shakily and lifted the Sharps rifle off Barr's shoulder. Barr shook his hand, as did Jim Flanagan, Joe Berger, and others. Horne thanked them.

Jim Dolittle walked up and shook his hand. "That was damn fine shooting, Marshal Horne. Thank you for what you've done here. If we're ever back this way, we'll look you up."

"Where you headed?" Barr asked.

"We got a claim needs mining out in California by next week, so duty calls. I like being with the Chinamen. They don't ask questions." With that, Dolittle released Horne's hand and left.

"What about the gold?" Asked one of the miners.

"Yes," said Edge Stevens. "Now that Kemp's dead, who gets his gold?" Some murmuring broke out amongst the townsfolk and miners about who was entitled to the claim. Suddenly, Horne reached into his pocket and pulled out a large gold nugget. He raised it up and let everyone see it.

"It's true!" Shouted Jessie Hayes.

Another miner spoke up. "I've not seen a nugget that size in my whole life!"

Horne interrupted the curiosity. "This isn't even the biggest piece. There's nuggets the size of your hands up in the gulch."

A general excitement rose, but that quickly gave way to arguing. Horne shouted them down.

"But...this isn't gold."

A murmur rose again, this time against Horne. Some were confused, others claimed he wanted it for himself, and some still believed it was gold.

"Not gold?" Barr scratched his unshaven face.

Horne pulled the nugget to his eye and inspected it. "This folks, is pyrite. It grows wild in all the surrounding rivers. Ask any old timer and you'll hear it by another name: fool's gold."

"So, that ain't even real gold?" Jessie Hayes inquired.

"Did Kemp know that?" Marv Turner asked.

"I don't know," Horne replied truthfully. "But it got you folks, and I suspect, that's all he needed. Had he lived, he would have seen the destruction of Talon's Crossing. Men like him are just out to destroy all that's good in this world."

"Not anymore," said Barr.

"Let's hear it for Marshal Gideon Horne!" Shouted Mayor Jim Flanagan, raising an arm. "Hip, hip..."

"Hooray!" Shouted the group.

✪✪✪

Days passed and the miners slowly left, paying back what they could to the local businessmen, who were more thankful for their help in eliminating Kemp and the others. The bodies of Slick Mark Johns, Cap Crawford, and Chauncey were buried in unmarked graves in the cemetery. Horne wrote to the governor describing what happened in Talon's Crossing. He wrote of the good that Crawford had done in his life, and asked that his one, final act not wholly judge who he was. On the other hand, Horne noted, our actions are all that can define us. He hoped now that the era of Slick Mark Johns could end and peace could return to Nevada.

Weeks later, Deputy Seth Barr entered the Marshal's Office. It was Saturday and he had the day off. Horne looked up to see him standing in the doorway with his wife, Alyssa, a young, curly-headed blonde with bright, green eyes. She had an arm around her husband.

"What brings you here on your day off, Seth?"

Barr stepped forward and handed him a letter. "Wanted to give you this in person. Got it yesterday after you lit out for home."

Horne looked at the address. It was from the governor's office. He quickly ripped it open and read it aloud:

"Marshal Gideon Horne: Thank you for your exceptional service to the town of Talon's Crossing, the county of Lander, and the state of Nevada. We are so lucky to have dedicated and skillful lawmen in that part of the country. Your apprehension of fugitive Mark Johns, his associates, and a two-way lawman will be recorded in official documents so all can know what's been done. I applaud your efforts. As you well know, Herman Crawford was a territorial marshal for Nevada, one of a dozen elite men tasked with dealing justice. If it pleases you, I would very much like to extend an offer for you to join this team. Now that there's an opening, I would be overjoyed to have a man of your caliber among their ranks. Please let me know how this pleases you. Gratefully yours, Jewett W. Adams, Governor of Nevada."

Horne hesitated before he set the letter down, taking it all in. He'd never planned to leave Talon's Crossing, but an offer like this only came once in a lifetime. To work for the governor himself, tracking down the most notorious outlaws in Nevada? He wasn't sure what he thought.

Seth Barr grinned. "So, are you gonna do it, Marshal?"

Horne thought it over. He wanted to do it, but also didn't want to leave Talon's Crossing. This was his home. He could always come back after a few seasons of work. Besides, Barr would make a great replacement.

"Maybe," he mused. "But I've got a few weeks until he needs an answer."

With that, Barr and his wife left for their Saturday picnic. Horne saddled up his mare in the corral, where she'd been resting, and rode her out to the mountain gulch where he'd been shot by Mark Johns. His shoulder was still sore, even after a few days, but it was improving. As he jumped her over the crevice, he swallowed hard, remembering the perilous climb up. He led Penny through the grove of pines until he reached the sparkling river. He dismounted, walked over to the water, and pulled the nugget from his vest pocket.

Horne had seen pyrite many times before, but this wasn't it. Pyrite wasn't nearly as heavy, nor did it melt as easily. Horne had tested the nugget in his office over the past few days and concluded that, in fact, it was gold. Either way, he figured, it was best that no one knew this was here. Like Johns and Crawford, bad men and trouble flocked to gold. For Talon's Crossing, a meager, yet peaceful, life was enough. As its protector, he knew he had to make the hard choices.

"It's for the best," said Horne and tossed the gold nugget back into the stream.

THE END

ABOUT OUR CREATORS

WRITER –

TYLER AUFFHAMMER - is the author of numerous works of fiction, nonfiction, and poetry, including 2018's *1950s Western Roundup*. His writing interests include westerns and pulp adventure stories. He is a graduate of Western Carolina University. Currently, he teaches English and creative writing in North Carolina, where he lives with his wife and dog.

INTERIOR ILLUSTRATOR –

JEFF CRAM - is a graduate of the Joe Kubert School of Cartoon and Graphic Art Inc. An illustrator and author with nearly twenty years of professional experience, he lives in Maine with his wife and two children. You can follow him on Instagram @cramnation.

COVER ARTIST -

ADAM BENET SHAW –Accomplished painter, illustrator, and comics creator, Adam has garnered acclaim across a number of artistic media. After completing studies at the Cleveland Institute of Art in Ohio, the Edinburgh College of Art in Scotland and Watts Atelier in California, Shaw was selected as an emerging American artist to watch by European gallery owners and exhibited in London, England. He has been featured in "New American Painting", selected multiple times for the Arkansas Art Center's Delta Exhibit, and shown at the prestigious "Red Clay Survey" at the Huntsville Museum of Art. His work has also been shown in over 50 group and solo shows in the US and internationally. His figurative paintings are a prominent part of a 140-foot mural entitled "The History of Cotton" at the National Cotton Exchange Museum, St. Jude's Children's Research Hospital, the National Contact Bridge Museum, and a treasured part of private and corporate collections. He has created storyboards for several motion pictures, including Paramount Pictures' film "Black Snake Moan" directed by Craig Brewer, stage design for operas and corporate events, and character illustrations for the gaming industry. His published graphic novel work includes the series "Dead In Memphis", "Bloodstream" for Image Comics, "David: The Illustrated Novel" from Shepherd King Publishing and "Harpe: America's First Serial Killers" from Cave-in-Rock Publishing. He shares his love of art through teaching and workshops at his studio in the Broad Avenue Arts District in Memphis. Recently he has been painting book covers for pulp publishers Pro Se Productions and Airship 27 Productions.

✪✪✪

TERROR ON THE PLAINS

Former Union scouts and saddle tramps Durken and McAfee are more than satisfied with their lives as cattle-punchers for Homer Eldridge and his Triple Six ranch. But fate has other, more sinister and weird plans for the two cowpokes...

Writer Fred Adams, Jr. spins weird western tales that will have readers on their edge of their seats and jumping at shadows. Mixing a heady brew that is half H.P. Lovecraft and half Louis L'Amour, SIX-GUN TERRORS volumes one through three are creepy adventures not soon forgotten.

HIS NAME WAS MANKILLER

Young Jason Mankiller never believed his surname was an omen of his future until the Civil War broke out and he joined the Union Army. Fate took him to the fields of Gettysburg. By the time the battle ended, he was sitting atop a small rise surrounded by the bodies of dozens of Confederate troopers. Days later, while drunk, his fellow soldiers had tears of blood tattooed onto his face. From that day forward, the Man Who Cried Blood's reputation spread far and wide.

Ten years later, Jason Mankiller is in Ft. Rogers, Texas, hoping to find a job and bury his past. But the blood tattoo won't let him escape the gunfighter's trail. Writer R.A. Jones delivers an old fashioned western adventure in the grand tradition of Max Brand and Louis L'Amour. Here are pioneering men and women facing the birth of a new American destiny that will demand their blood, sweat, tears and sacrifice. For Jason Mankiller, that promise of a better life will be claimed at the end of a smoking gun.

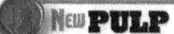